Tell Me the Truth
About Love

BOOKS BY MARY CABLE

FICTION

Tell Me the Truth About Love   1991

Avery's Knot   1981

NONFICTION

The Blizzard of '88   1988

Top Drawer:
American High Society from the Gilded Age
to the Roaring Twenties   1984

Lost New Orleans   1980

The Little Darlings:
A History of Child-Rearing in America   1975

El Escorial   1971

Black Odyssey:
The Case of the Slaveship Amistad   1971

The Avenue of the Presidents   1969

American Manners and Morals   1969

Dream Castles   1966

Tell Me the Truth About Love

About Love

✦

MARY CABLE

ATHENEUM • NEW YORK • 1991

Collier Macmillan Canada
Toronto

Maxwell Macmillan International
New York • Oxford • Singapore • Sydney

Fic
CAB

This is a work of fiction. Names, characters, places, and incidents either are the product of the author's imagination or are used fictitiously. Any resemblance to events or persons, living or dead, is entirely coincidental.

Atheneum
Macmillan Publishing Company
866 Third Avenue, New York, NY 10022

Collier Macmillan Canada, Inc.
1200 Eglinton Avenue East, Suite 200
Don Mills, Ontario M3C 3N1

Library of Congress Cataloging-in-Publication Data
Cable, Mary.
Tell me the truth about love / Mary Cable.
p. cm.
ISBN 0-689-11871-6
I. Title.
PS3553.A27T45   1991
813'.54--dc20   90-48853   CIP

DESIGNED BY ERICH HOBBING

10 9 8 7 6 5 4 3 2 1

Printed in the United States of America

To
Harriet Wasserman
With love and appreciation

Will it come like a change in the weather?
Will its greeting be courteous or rough?
Will it alter my life altogether?
O tell me the truth about love.

W. H. AUDEN
("Twelve Songs," # XII)

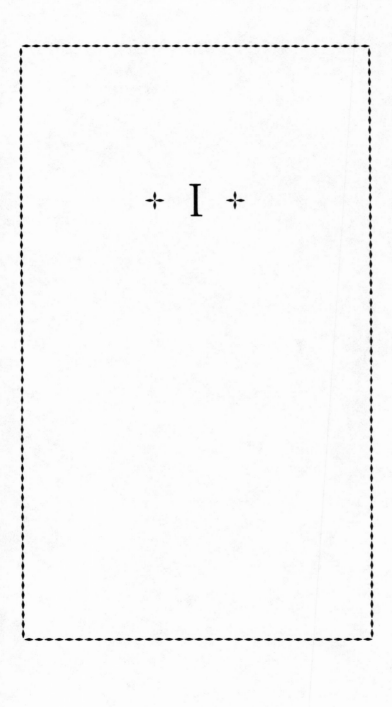

I

A headline, "Smithson Family Feud," in the Santa Fe *New Mexican* one May morning several years ago, led to the changing of my entire life. At the time I did not foresee any changes, even small ones. I had been Mrs. Osgood Decatur Smithson IV for eighteen years, and, as my mother would have put it, I was well-fixed. Whenever I felt depressed, as I often did, I tried hard to remind myself that I lived in a beautiful part of the world, surrounded by chili fields and peace and quiet, and that I really had no problems except an oppressive mother-in-law; into each life some rain must fall.

On that landmark morning, Oz left for his bank directly after breakfast, as usual. He had a routine that never varied: up at seven, push-ups, shower, dressing; bran cereal, wheat germ, skim milk, coffee, and a handful of vitamin pills; yesterday's *Wall Street Journal* propped against the fern on the breakfast table. At twenty to eight he was out the door, so that he would arrive at his bank in Santa Fe close to an hour before its doors were opened.

I usually puttered around the kitchen, still in my bathrobe, until he said, "I'm leaving, Alex." Then I said, " 'Bye, Oz." A kiss was not part of this procedure, and I was glad about that. I had seen other husbands and wives go through a kiss-good-bye ritual, and it didn't necessarily mean love; nor did Oz's inert "I'm leaving" mean nonlove. I believed he loved me, and I considered him a nice man.

That morning, as soon as he had driven away, I wandered down the drive to the mailbox in order to pick up the morning paper. We lived in the country outside Santa Fe, where you look at mountains in almost every direction. That day, the highest peaks still had snow on them, but here in the valley it was full spring. The early morning air was drenched with sunlight, and every little pebble in the road had an important ink-black shadow. A bull snake crossed in front of me, leaving an elegant curved track in the dust. When I first came to live in New Mexico, snakes made me scream. Now I had learned to admire their grace and their purposeful glide. They seemed to know where they were going, and that was a quality I envied.

Back at the house, I poured a second cup of coffee and returned to bed with it and the paper. No one knew that I liked to do this. "Idle, lazy, decadent" I often told myself, but then I'd say, "Why not?" I have no children, no job, and no demands on me other than picking up the cleaning woman once a week and shopping and cooking and tidying. In behalf of tidying, I always made up Oz's twin bed before returning into my own. There, I glanced at the headlines and then browsed through the death notices, the police blotter, and Ann Landers.

On that particular morning I had intended to read a canto of *The Divine Comedy*, getting ready for the advanced Italian class I was taking.

"Why Italian?" Oz had asked when I first started studying it.

"Because I loved it when I was a little girl. When Daddy was in the Consulate in Florence."

My Foreign Service childhood was of no interest to Oz. He had been to Europe once, on a family tour, and did not care to go again.

"But Italian is of no use to you now. Why not learn something useful?"

Given the difference in our personalities, there was no way to explain to him that I loved reading about Hell in a beautiful and subtle language.

So I said, "Why do you like to hunt?"

After a moment's thought, he said, "It can be exciting, and it makes me feel independent. It's nice to do something you know how to do."

"Then you know what Italian does for me," I said, and that ended the discussion.

> *In the middle of the journey of our life*
> *I found myself in a dark wood*
> *And at a loss to find the path ahead . . .*

Dante went on to say that he was frightened, and that he had no idea how he had come to such a place. When I first read these lines, I felt certain that, difficult though I found it, I must go on with *La Divina Commedia.* I knew what Dante was talking about.

But on that May morning, I never did read my Dante assignment, or Ann Landers, either. I had only just noticed, in the morning newspaper, the startling headline "Smithson Family Feud," when the telephone rang and I heard the gravelly, constant-smoker voice of my mother-in-law, Lydia Smithson.

Dispensing with amenities such as "Good morning," she demanded, "Have you seen the paper?"

"I've only just opened it."

"You're in for a nasty surprise, Alexandra. The photographer and the reporter came to see me two days ago. I must say, I think it's shocking that the reporter woman couldn't get the facts straight, because I was very clear. She's written that I was a debutante in 1928. *Any*body could tell you I was still a schoolgirl at Farmington in 1928. And the photograph is terrible of both Deck and me. Makes us look a hundred. It's good of the Gilbert Stuart, though."

While listening to this, which made no sense to me, I glanced through the lead paragraph of the article. It said that David Smithson, younger son of Mr. and Mrs. Osgood Decatur Smithson III, was suing to obtain guardianship of his parents on the grounds that they were habitual drunkards and of unsound mind; and also because they were attempting to bequeath their property, the Gallegos Ranch, with its Spanish-Colonial adobe houses, to a religious organization called Glorious Light rather than to their two sons.

"Deck and I only found out last week what David is trying to do," Lydia went on. "It was such a shock to me that I went to bed. Can you imagine *David* doing such a dreadful thing? To *us*?"

I thought, but didn't say, that yes, I could imagine it. David—handsome, clever, energetic David—had always been Lydia's favorite child, but of recent years their relationship had been bumpy. Her buoyant expectations that he would become a tycoon, or a senator, or some other kind of very important man, had gradually given way to disappointment. He was a cattle rancher, and not a very successful one at that.

"Alex, I suppose," Lydia went on nastily, "that

7

you and Oz have known all along about what David was plotting."

"The first I knew of it was five minutes ago," I said. "I didn't know, either, that you had made this new will."

"Turn to page nine. That's where the photograph of us is, and our side of the story, although I am totally amazed they left out so much of what I took the trouble to tell them. It seems that the reporter woman telephoned Oz and he declined comment, wouldn't you know, he avoids a confrontation whenever he can. Then she called David and he slandered me."

I put the receiver down for a moment while I turned to page nine. "I need time to read all this," I said to Lydia. "It's three full columns."

"After you've read them, I'll tell you what they should have said. I've just called Oz at the bank and he promised to come home this morning. I want you both over here for lunch."

"What time?" I asked, without enthusiasm.

"Early. Can you make it by eleven-thirty? We'll all be needing a little drinkie-poo."

Lydia had developed a frivolous social manner to the point where she seemed to be made of it. In the midst of a major family upheaval, she could speak of drinkie-poos.

"We'll come over as soon as we can," I said, trying to sound very calm, although I was trembling.

As soon as I had hung up, the phone rang again and the caller was a casual friend of mine, who had read the morning paper and was obviously after the inside story. I said that if she had read the paper she knew more than I did.

"Well, you must feel terrible about losing your house," she said.

The question was like an alarm bell in my head. Lose my house?

"I'll call you back later," I said, "after I'm sure what this is all about."

After that, I decided not to answer any more calls—the phone rang all morning—and I sat down to read the article carefully.

Yes, it was true. David was trying legally to obtain guardianship of his parents and to have the court set aside their new will, which left the Gallegos Ranch to Glorious Light. In fact, Decatur and Lydia Smithson had already given the Glorious Light people a deed, and David was asking the court to declare it void because of his parents' incompetency. David was also accusing Glorious Light of having exerted undue influence, which they had denied, declaring, "The Smithsons' offer came as a total surprise. We are willing to return the deed if they wish it, but Mrs. Smithson has urged us to defend the suit."

In response to an invitation from Mrs. Smithson, the newspaper had sent a reporter to talk to her.

"Among the many problems on her mind" (the reporter had written) "is the fear that if the property is left to one or both of her sons, they will sell it to developers." She was quoted as saying, "Neither of our boys has enough money to live here and keep the place up, and they would squabble over what to do with it. They might not be able to resist the temptation to sell it, and then this beautiful old hacienda would become a bingo hall and these exquisite, empty six hundred acres would be a subdivision. The whole Santa Fe charm thing that we have tried all these years to preserve would be down the drain."

When I had finished reading all this, I went through the motions of getting dressed while I thought and thought about it. The new will seemed bizarre indeed, and David's legal action even more so. But clearly both will and lawsuit were realities, and so was the distinct danger that Oz and I would have to move from this snug old adobe, where we had lived for eighteen years, or nearly half my life. Before that, I had moved often and far, since my father was a Foreign Service Officer. I grew up feeling deprived of a real home, and now the threat of losing this one stirred very old emotions.

It was after eleven o'clock that morning before I heard Oz's car in the driveway. Meanwhile, my rising anger had been fueled by a new thought:

Why wasn't I told? How can so much go on right under my nose and nobody bothers to tell me?

I knew, of course, that Lydia didn't consider me a full-fledged Smithson, but only a sort of concubine; that was because she hadn't picked me out herself as she had picked out David's wife, Bishy, the daughter of an old school friend in Brookline, Mass. The four parents had connived to throw the two together and bring about a marriage that could not have been more cunningly planned if they had all been Hapsburgs.

Old Decatur had always liked me, and in earlier years he had sometimes confided in me, but now he was too far gone in drink. As for David, we had hardly had a conversation in years, and Bishy had always made it clear that she didn't like me much. But Oz! Why had he said nothing? I went to the door to meet him.

"Oz, what is all this?" I rather sharply demanded.

He got out of his car slowly and came toward me, wearing what I call his sea-captain's face. We have a portrait of a nautical Smithson ancestor who looks very much like Oz. The captain's face, like Oz's, is bony and long, and his expression is wary, as if he has seen a pirate ship on the horizon. When I see Oz with his ancestor's expression, I invariably feel like cheering him up, soothing him, and convincing him that the pirates aren't there.

"I suppose you're mad at me, Alex," he said. "I

11

know I should have told you. It must have been hard on you, reading all this in the newspaper."

"Yes, it was, but never mind now, Oz. Just tell me your version."

"My version is that it's a mess. Pure and simple. I never dreamed David would do this."

"But did you know he was thinking about it?"

"Well, he called me a while back and asked if I'd go with him to see a lawyer. He wanted us to try for joint custody of Mother and Dad. I said no."

Oz edged past me into the house and sat down in his big chair. With a heavy sigh, he said, "I really didn't think he'd do this alone. Honest! Never dreamed it."

It crossed my mind that he had never dreamed it because he is not the type to dream, or imagine, or even consider possibilities. All his life he has been surprised by the devious ways of human beings. He is brilliant with figures, and he makes a fine and conscientious third vice-president of his bank, but he will never be its president because of this failure to anticipate shenanigans and foibles. He would be sure to make bad loans.

But I knew he couldn't help it. I knew that there was no use in scolding or lecturing him, any more than one would scold a tree for dropping its leaves in autumn. It was his nature and I had learned to live with it. Oz and I never experienced fireworks of joy, but no black abysses either. Our hours together were punctuated by the sound of rustling newspapers, spoons in the soup, and voices on the television. Oz is fifty now, and has more or less always been fifty. He believes in his own generation and that of his parents, and in his placid career as a vice-president of his admirably solvent bank. And these things keep him feeling that he knows what's right.

I said, "What about the will? Surely there's still something in it for you, isn't there?"

"Yes, some stocks and bonds, but I'm afraid Dad has run through most of them. His only really important possession is the ranch."

There was a short silence, while I took in the implications of all this. I had been looking forward to a lot of money one day, after Lydia and Decatur had been called heavenward. In idle moments I had daydreamed about renting a villa in Italy or a flat in London; or going to New York every winter, in order to take courses and see plays.

"My God, Oz," I said, and sank down on the sofa. The newspaper was open to the photograph, and I looked at it again, feeling that I might see two monsters pictured there. Instead, I was struck by how poised and calm both Lydia and Deck appeared. Lydia was wearing her best country-lady clothes: cashmere and tweed and an heirloom brooch of pearls and amethysts. Deck, in his English jacket with leather elbows, leaned back in his

13

chair, jauntily balancing a highball on his knee. It was true that they appeared old, even ancient; but the kind of ancient that comes from a lifetime of self-assurance and of having things their way. I was reminded of Egyptian Pharaohs, getting as much or more attention after becoming mummies than most living people. I had the feeling that Lydia and Deck's new will was a pharaonic device for continuing to run things even from beyond the grave. And never mind what the rest of us might want or feel.

"Oz, the whole story is outrageous," I said. "And how did these Glorious Light people get involved? I never heard of them."

"Mother was taken in by some girl who came around asking for contributions," he said. "She says the girl was so sweet and sincere and conservatively dressed. Then it turned out that she was related to the Berry family in Hartford and the Berrys are some sort of cousins of ours. Also, she promised never to poison the prairie dogs. So when she asked for a contribution—"

"—Lydia contributed the Gallegos Ranch!"

"Right. David thinks she was probably drunk. He says she and Dad are never sober these days."

"That's not true. They're sober in the mornings. But how would David know, anyway? He hasn't been to see them in ages."

"Mrs. Martinez told him."

Mrs. Martinez was housekeeper for the elder Smithsons. I wondered why she hadn't confided in Oz, but then I realized that she probably preferred David. Most people did.

Oz went on, "Mother told me she doesn't trust David, or me either, not to sell this place to developers. She imagines a fake adobe suburb here, and about six malls. The cottonwoods will be cut down, along with every piñon tree. And the pond will be drained and the ducks won't stop here anymore. So that's why they changed the will."

"And disinherited their heirs," I said, my voice trembling. "I don't know, Oz—maybe David is right. This doesn't seem rational."

But Oz looked disapproving. "He's wrong, Alex. Dead wrong to drag our parents through the courts. Bishy agrees. I told him the only right way to handle this is to talk them out of it. That's what I intend to do, but he doesn't want to bother. He never comes here, I guess because he doesn't want to see them. I don't know what's wrong with him."

"He's acting like a son-of-a-bitch, that's what's wrong with him," I burst out.

Oz looked surprised by my sudden vehemence. "Maybe *you* could talk him out of it," he said. "You and he used to be pretty good friends."

"I don't want to talk to him," I said. "No, Oz, it's up to you. You talk to your mother, and Deck will go along, I'm sure. Come on, they'll be waiting for us."

We walked across the acre of lawn that lies between the house we lived in and Oz's parents', known as the main house. In New Mexico, a lawn is a luxury, requiring constant attention and watering, but Lydia had always insisted on having one. For her it is a sign of civilization, and she would as soon go without clothes as without a lawn.

We let ourselves in at the handsome carved front door, which is worn and weathered and entering its third century. The brass doorknocker, in the shape of a pineapple, was brought from Lydia's girlhood home in Providence, Rhode Island. It, too, is old, with about two hundred years of polishing on it. I have sometimes idly wondered how much that doorknocker can be polished before it fades like an old star and disappears altogether. Now, as Oz and I walked into the house, it occurred to me that it was the Smithsons who were disappearing. The knocker would long outlast them.

Lydia has a passion for handsome antiques. It is second only to her passion for endangered species. Human beings come in third. This house is a treasure trove of Spanish-Colonial objects, which Lydia "picked up" during the Depression from poor and hungry families in the Santa Fe area. Besides the New Mexican things, she and Deck also own several museum-quality heirlooms from both their families, now damaged by the New Mexican climate, which is too dry for them. There is a Newport highboy and a wing chair with mahogany feet carved to look like a lion's. These two pieces had seen Lydia come and they would see her go; and when she goes, they will be shipped back East again as bequests to the Rhode Island School of Design.

The old adobe house is a treasure in itself, but Lydia and Deck, still New Englanders at heart, respect but do not love its Hispanic look. The front door leads into a *sala*, with built-in *bancos* around the walls, made less unpleasantly hard by Navajo and Rio Grande blankets. Carved wooden saints crowd the mantelpiece, and whenever Lydia and Deck have a party, they light votive candles in front of them.

But Lydia and Deck do not live in the *sala*. They prefer the cluttered hominess of their library, with its worn chintz-covered chairs and matching chintz curtains, and hundreds of old copies of the *National Geographic* piled on the bookshelves, along with an encyclopedia and shabby sets of Dickens and Hugh Walpole.

"Ooo-hoo! Here we are!" I sang out, in the false and simpleminded manner that I knew Lydia liked.

"Ooo-hoo!" came Lydia's voice.

An aged West Highland terrier, Belinda, impeded the way into the library by lying across the threshold. She had been doing this for about fifteen years, and from time to time visitors had tripped over her and entered the room sprawling. But Lydia believed that Belinda was guarding the castle keep, in obedience to some archaic and aristocratic instinct. Oz and I automatically found a way around her.

Lydia and Deck sat in wing chairs on each side of the fireplace—where, in spite of the mild May weather outside, a fire was blazing. Looking down from the mantel was Decatur's great-great-grandmother, painted by Gilbert Stuart. She was a pretty young woman, dressed in yellow satin, with a yellow satin turban in the style of the 1790s, and she looked confident of her good looks and her elegance. Not for her the indignities of the candid camera.

Deck had made a shaker of martinis and he and his wife had it between them, on a low, rickety table that was strewn with mail-order catalogues. There was also the morning *New Mexican*.

Lydia pointed to it angrily as she said, "I just would like to know what you think of a son who would do a thing like this."

"I think it's terrible, Ma," Oz said.

"I'm glad to hear you say that," Lydia said, scrutinizing him sharply. "I was wondering whether you were in on it."

"Certainly not. I told David not to do it."

"Daddy's heart is broken," Lydia said. We all looked at Decatur, who nodded. His arthritic old hand shook, but held on to the eighteenth-century goblet in which he liked to drink his martinis.

"Needless to say, my heart is broken as well," his wife went on. "But I'm a fighter. David won't get away with this. I've already talked to Bishy. Tracked her down, visiting her mother in the East. She thinks David must have waited until she was safely out of the state before he sicked his lawyer on us."

Oz went to the bar and assembled the makings of a Bloody Mary. And, although I am not much of a drinker, I said I'd have one, too.

Deck said to Lydia, "Darling, you didn't tell me you'd talked to Bishy."

Lydia cast her eyes heavenward. "I *did* tell you," she said. "You just forgot. You see"—she turned to Oz—"You see, it is true, your father does forget. But that doesn't mean he's loony. And neither am I."

"Of course not, Ma."

"We're old and we're down, but we're not out."

"Certainly not."

"Bishy says not to worry. She says she's working on a plan, and she'll be flying back to New Mexico in a few days. And we're not to say anything to David, because she intends to come to Santa Fe first and talk to me."

"What's the plan, Ma?"

"She wouldn't tell me over the phone. But she said not to worry, and she usually knows what she's talking about." Lydia took a swig of her martini, found a bottle of olives on the floor beside her chair, and popped two olives into her glass. Then she added, addressing no one in particular, "Bishy has been wonderful. Ever since she married David, it's been as if she were my very own daughter."

My adrenalin surged, but I said nothing. I was used to this kind of remark from Lydia, and had been since the day I met him.

After Lydia had had her second martini, she began to weep. I couldn't remember ever having seen her do such a thing before, except the time that Belinda's predecessor, a Skye terrier, had been carried off by an eagle. Tears rolled down her furrowed cheeks and she rocked back and forth. "David—" she said gaspingly. "Little Davey—"

I felt sure that in her mind's eye she was seeing a beautiful, energetic two-year-old, not a tired-eyed forty-six-year-old man. But I could not help but think of "Absalom, my son, my son—" and in spite of my dislike for her, I was moved to say, "Not to worry" (since this phrase of Bishy's had seemed to be a comfort). "We'll get him to change his mind."

She looked at me as if she would like to believe me, but couldn't. "Well, I thank you for the thought, but how do *you* know? Maybe you think you know him, but believe me he's changed a lot since—when was it?—that New Year's Eve you came out here from New York because he'd asked you. You probably thought he was easy to push around, and he was, I suppose. Especially by girls. But he's changed." And she closed her eyes and dabbed them with a wadded-up Kleenex.

Her husband was peering at her in some distress. She was obviously embarrassing him.

"What about lunch, darling?" he asked.

"Lunch?" The word seemed unfamiliar to her. Then she said, "Oh! Lunch!" And collecting herself, smoothed her hair. "Mrs. Martinez said she'd put sandwiches on the table, and some salad. It's all probably ready. Let's bring our drinks."

Lydia ran her household in a picnicky kind of way, but the picnic had a certain shabby elegance. Mrs. Martinez, now assisted by her daughter Filomena, had been with the Smithsons since their first days in New Mexico, when the boys were small. Entertaining had been Lydia's forte. Mrs. Martinez still set the table with the Porthault linen place mats, now mended and slightly brown here and there with hot-iron marks put there by the inept Filomena. But instead of five- or six-course dinners, with finger bowls at the end, Lydia and Deck lived on sandwiches and salad for lunch and one course—say, lamb chops and frozen spinach—for dinner. When we walked into the dining room that particular day, four places were set with Spode plates and Baccarat crystal, with a Venetian glass bowl of tulips as a centerpiece, but the menu was ham and cheese sandwiches and a salad of iceberg lettuce.

By the time we sat down, Lydia had recovered her poise and was once again talking inanities. It seemed as if she wished to forget the matter at hand.

"Have your Emperor tulips bloomed yet, Alex?" she asked me. "You never seem to have much luck with tulips."

A tanager, on a branch just outside the dining-room window, was intent on hawthorn berries.

"Hey, a western tanager," said Decatur, interrupting his wife. "The red head—yellow body—black and white wings—by golly, rare to see at this altitude."

"Not rare," said Oz. "He's probably headed north from wherever he spends the winter."

"Where is that?" Lydia asked.

"I don't know."

"Don't know? I thought you were the big Audubon Society supporter." She picked up her fork and angrily stabbed a hunk of lettuce.

I came to Oz's rescue. "They all go to Central America, don't they, dear?"

"But *where* in Central America?" Lydia demanded.

The tanager hopped to another branch, peered through the window at us, and then, as if horrified, took wing.

"Get the bird book, Oz," his mother said.

I thought, she's forgotten that years have gone by since meals here had to be instructive. From Oz I had heard that when he and David were growing up, Lydia had insisted on teaching them something while they were captive at the table. Where is Turkistan? Get the atlas. What is the meaning of "symbiosis"? Get the dictionary. She liked to say now that she had helped both of them get into Harvard. Maybe, I thought, but she had also made both of them eat too fast and bolt from the table.

Decatur offered wine to Oz and me—we declined —and then filled his own glass. Lydia had brought her third prelunch martini to the table with her.

"Put a little more gin in this for me, Oz dear."

"Mother," Oz said, "let's not forget why you asked us to lunch."

"Of course not. That's why I need more gin."

Oz glumly fetched it for her. Of his family, he was the only one who didn't drink much. I was grateful not to have *that* problem with him, but I also saw that sobriety separated him from the kind of fun the others had—or used to have, anyway.

High jinks. Larks. Revelry. At times like this—
stressful times—these two tried to revive it. A deep
red flush had come across Lydia's wrinkled face
and her handsome dark eyes glittered. One could
see traces of the beauty she had once had. A photograph of her in the library showed her as a bride,
circa 1930, her arms full of freesia and white roses,
her turned-back veil making a gentle snowstorm all
about her head. Miss Lydia Aspinwall must have
been the Bachrach photographer's idea of a perfect
bride. He had posed her meekly gazing at the
flowers, her face totally without expression. Blank.
A blank bride had been the ideal.

I thought of my own parents, who had also been
married in the early 1930s, but without the help of
Bachrach or a wedding dress or even roses. I have
a snapshot of them standing on the steps of New
York City Hall: Fielding Burrows, my father, wearing a double-breasted pinstripe suit with a white
chrysanthemum in the buttonhole; and Alice, his
bride, in a practical navy blue suit and a matching
hat that had a small white bow on it. What they
lacked in style they made up for with eager smiles.
They were full of plans and ambitions. Already
Fielding was on the lowest rung in the State
Department, a junior Foreign Service Officer, and
they were about to go off to their first post, Dutch
Guiana. Whereas Lydia and her bridegroom had
had no plans at all beyond moving into the twenty-

eight room Smithson house on Angell Street in Providence, and spending summers at Narragansett. When, several years later, they moved to Santa Fe to safeguard Deck's delicate lungs, it was their first and last adventure.

"Here's your gin, Mother," Oz said. "But please eat your lunch. We're going to have to talk sensibly."

"What I want to know is," Lydia said, straightening her back and looking stately, "where do *you* stand in this outrage?"

He sighed. "It's simple. After you changed your will in favor of the Glorious Lighters, David came to me and said he'd been talking to his lawyer and—"

"—What lawyer?" put in Decatur. "Is it Ollie Fain? I've known him since he was five years old. He was retarded then and he's retarded now."

"Maybe so, Dad, but he's a pretty shrewd lawyer. He reminded David about that accident you had in Santa Fe last year, when you finally lost your license. Now he and David are using that to show you're non compos mentis."

"I've been driving sixty-five years and this whippersnapper judge takes my license. A damned outrage and David knows it. I taught David to drive."

"Oh, don't, *don't* talk about David's driving," Lydia cried. And we all thought of David's terrible accident, twelve years earlier. Driving too fast on a two-lane country road, he had run full-speed into a rickety pickup emerging from an unmarked wagontrack. The pickup driver was critically injured but survived; David's injuries were minor, except for a fractured leg, and Bishy wasn't along. But their four-year-old son, their only child, who had been standing on the seat beside his father, was killed instantly. Yes, no matter how angry we might be with David, it was cruel to mention his driving.

Decatur continued hastily, "I made a mistake, but I shouldn't have lost my license."

"Dad, you turned left when you should have turned right and somebody's adobe wall had to be replaced. But never mind that. Your doctor will vouch for you that you're not senile."

"He'd better! Fortman has been our doctor since the days when doctors made house calls. Delivered Oz, I think, didn't he, Lydia?"

"Fortman? I don't think so. Anyway, he's dead."

"What? Ed Fortman dead?" Decatur looked stricken. "Nobody told me."

"Died four years ago, Deck. Your doctor now is Humphreys, but you don't like him."

"No. He's a whippersnapper."

Oz said, "Humphreys is fine, Dad. I'll talk to him. We'll get affidavits."

"You're a comfort, Oz," Lydia said. "I'm glad you're on our side."

"Wait a minute," Oz said. "I have news for

you, Ma. I'm not on your side." We all stared at
him, because he very seldom took such a solemn
and assertive stand. "I don't like what David is
doing, but I don't like what you are doing, either.
Why are you taking me out of your will?"

His voice went higher, which, despite his rigid
self-control, tells me that he is fighting against
rage.

"Because you have no children," Lydia said bit-
terly. "You and David don't care about *family*,
and there are no heirs to carry on the name here.
You and David would sell to—"

"Yes, I know—developers. David might. I
wouldn't."

"David is very strong," said Lydia. "He always
could get anything out of you, even when you
were children. You'd let him ride your horse, borrow your camera—and as for Alex, she thinks he's
the cat's pajamas."

"I don't!" I burst out. Maybe too vehemently.

"Cat's pajamas! Ma, what 1920s' funny paper
did you get that one out of?" Oz said crossly.
"We all know what David is like—he's selfish,
self-serving, self-absorbed. We'll get you the best
lawyer in town and we'll collect affidavits, and
David can jump in the lake."

"Splendid!" Decatur cried, raising his glass.
"You've saved us, Oz. That's the end of it."

But Lydia shook her head. "David *never* jumps

in the lake. Not when he is really set on something."

"Nonsense," said her husband. "He used to flit from one thing to another. You used to tell him he was a grasshopper and Oz was the ant."

"That was when he was young and foolish. Now he's middle-aged—"

"—And foolish," Oz said.

"Yes, but very stubborn. You'll see."

"There's that bird again," said Decatur. The tanager was back for a few more of last winter's hawthorn berries.

"Get the bird book, Deck," Lydia said. "I'll prove to you that's no western tanager. It's a grosbeak."

"I have to get back to the bank now," Oz said, throwing down his napkin. "I'm going to help you, but I'm terribly disappointed that you don't want to leave this place to your descendants. Please think it over. Good-bye."

We left them still at the table, toying with their sandwiches. Deck was looking up the tanager.

As we walked back across the lawn, Oz said, "I don't know—maybe they *are* senile."

I felt a wave of sympathy for Oz, as near as I could come to true closeness with him. Most of the time I had no idea what he was thinking or feeling, and long ago I had given up trying. But at rare times like these, I could tell how emotional he felt, and I found it very sad that he had to keep it to himself. I took his hand, but it was limp and unresponsive.

"I'm going back to the office," he said and walked away toward his car.

I thought, Lydia and Deck have not changed a bit since I've known them, but now that something so unthinkable has happened, more happenings will follow. It's as if a stone in an old wall had suddenly shifted. When it moves, so do others. Things will begin to slide about now, and there's no knowing where they'll go.

❖ II ❖

"Alexandra is from away," Lydia was apt to say when she introduced me to anyone. "From away" was a phrase she learned as a child in Rhode Island, where indigenous Rhode Islanders often use it to describe persons not from there. It bears a faint suggestion that something is wrong with such persons.

In my case, though, "away" is truly where I come from. Being a Foreign Service child, I am not "from" anywhere—certainly not from my birthplace, which happens to have been Uruguay. I also seem to be from away in connection with Time. By that I don't mean crazy. I mean that although I am perfectly aware of what century this is and I know that I was born close to the middle of it, I was brought up in the manners and sensitivities and expectations of the 1930s and 1920s and even earlier. This was because my parents were "older parents"; my father was forty-two and my mother thirty-nine when I was born. They already had an eight-year-old daughter, my sister Ginevra, and they had not planned another child. Because they lived away from the United States, American culture shocks largely passed them by, and they raised me like a child of times now thoroughly outmoded. I always had a nanny (or *kindermädchen* or ayah, depending on what part of the globe we were in), I ate separately from my parents, and I was carefully trained in matters no longer of importance except in the diplomatic service: for example, the proper lengths of white gloves, the use of calling cards, and where to sit in a room if you are the lowest-ranking person there (never on the sofa).

I also learned that Ginevra and I were here on earth for the advancement of our father, Fielding Burrows. Our mother told us stories of children who had disgraced their fathers by failing to be nice to everybody, particularly to foreigners, whose right to their own weird habits must be respected; or by throwing a tantrum in public or otherwise behaving like an Ugly American. Don't criticize! Be a good listener! And if this meant listening patiently while some unreconstructed Nazi gave excuses for Hitler, then that's what you had to do—just like Dad and Mother.

I learned these lessons and became very cautious about expressing opinions or even having them. My father used to say, "I'm of two minds" or "I need to sleep on it," and, as a rule, so do I. But when *he* felt cornered, he could point to some State Department directive or regulation. "I regret that we cannot help you," he might tell a terrified American beatnik, arrested in Turkey with traces of marijuana in his pockets. "Unfortunately, according to Regulation I-415 . . ." Or, to a Rumanian national in Istanbul, desperate to immigrate to the United States on the next plane, "There is a ten-year wait, but the guidelines permit me to take your name."

Although I was fourteen when my father died, I have few vivid memories of him. He always worked early and late at the Consulate or Embassy, and came home either to go out with my mother to parties, to host one, or to go to bed. On weekends, he liked to sit and read piles of newspapers. He was definitely not the sort of father who would teach you how to throw and catch, or take you fishing. As the years went by, the good food at parties got the better of him and he was subject to dyspepsia. My mother often used to tell me, "Don't bother Daddy—he's not feeling up to snuff." And in Bangkok, where nineteen kinds of salmonella were a continual menace, he once had to be taken to the hospital directly from a Queen's Birthday reception at the British Embassy.

I have a photograph of the three of us (my sister was at college in the States). We are on the wide veranda of the Bangkok house where we lived, surrounded by many empty rattan chairs. That indicated that we had had a party the night before and the extra chairs hadn't been put away yet. Daddy sat in one of them, reading. One could hardly see his face, because the Bangkok *Post* was in front of most of it. Mother was in another chair, some distance away, smiling for the camera. She was always good at that: social smiles, smiles saying cheese, were a genuine talent with her. She was a pretty woman, with curly light hair and gray-blue eyes that looked guileless. (I look like her, but not guileless; more evasive, I'd say.) In this photograph, I am thirteen. I am seated on the veranda steps, holding up a chinchook (one of Bangkok's ubiquitous house lizards) and squinting at the sun. I am smiling, too, but I have not developed the art of camera smiles and the look on my face is more of a grimace. I think the gardener, Sampong, was holding the camera. I don't remember much about him, except that he was thin, with a shiny light brown face, and always wore, as his complete costume, a baggy white loincloth. Probably he was smiling, too. Thais smile a lot. But his personality blurs in my memory with other men servants we had here and there. Outstanding is the blue-black one, in Africa, in his pristine white garments and perky white hat, and his dignified manner that my mother complained was somehow condescending.

This photograph of three disconnected souls on a Bangkok veranda haunts me. Only the rattan chairs, side by side with their wide arms nudging, or tipped up against one another, seem convivial.

I remember very clearly the first party my parents gave after we arrived in Bangkok, a seated dinner for thirty, with the tables set on the lawn. Each table was lit by candles and adorned by flowers arranged in the Thai manner—many blossoms closely packed (one might say jammed) into small vases. A circle of rosebuds might surround a circle of jasmine, and in the middle would be large, fullblown roses, as many as possible. Unlike the reticent Japanese arrangements, where every flower counts, Thai bouquets give the effect of unfailing abundance, of tropical gardens where nothing ever seems to stop growing. To those of us from cold countries, where philodendrons live humbly in small pots, it seems strange to see these same plants sprawling and climbing higher than our heads.

My parents soon learned not to give seated dinners in Thailand, because sometimes the Thai guests would simply never show up (they had preferred another invitation), or they would arrive bringing friends and relatives. Western-style party planning apparently seemed rigid to them. And, beautiful though that lawn party was, old Bangkok hands warned that snakes come out after nightfall and that some of these snakes are cobras, kraits, and pythons. Now, when I recall that evening, with the candlelight flickering on the flowers and the pleasant ebb and flow of voices, I imagine that the dark lawn beneath the guests' feet is invaded by swiftly slithering shapes. I wrote in my diary (at thirteen I had a taste for the melodramatic), "The party was paradise on top and sudden death under the tables."

The servants would have been no help in case of a cobra alarm, being Buddhists and reluctant to kill anything. When my mother encountered some large, villainous-looking insect inside the house, she would scream for Sampong, who would then come and tenderly carry it outside where it might enjoy a flower bed.

Since Bangkok is suffocatingly hot and humid nearly all the year round, the American Embassy allotted an air conditioner to each of its families. Ours was in the parental bedroom, so that (my mother told me) Dad could have a good sleep and do a good job at the office. My room had screened windows across three sides. Although it was next door to my parents, their closed door and windows and the hum of the air conditioner made me feel lonely and left out. Sleeping in my many-windowed room was almost like being in the trees, where leaves stirred in the night breezes, and from dark to dawn a miniature dinosaur—a gecko—crawled about the branches and spoke from time to time in a harsh and critical voice. He reminded me of an angry old man, carping about the food and the service.

I felt frightened, but of something beyond the night creatures; something beyond burglars or snakes or even the spirits that lived in the doll-size spirit house at the end of the garden and whom the servants propitiated with gifts of food and flowers. Perhaps I was frightened—and overwhelmed—by the continual changes in my life, and by the need to please so many people in so many different languages and by getting accustomed to one set of circumstances and then suddenly having them change to something quite different. In the several schools I had been to, I never got to be an old girl. My parents pointed out that all Foreign Service children had the same problems and that I had just better face up to them.

My father died in Bangkok. I say "died" because that was the word my mother preferred. In fact, he was murdered.

That was long before the time of worldwide terrorism, so the motive was not suspected of being political. The murderer was only an ordinary Thai burglar, clumsy enough to wake my parents in spite of the loud-humming air conditioner in their bedroom; and handy enough with a long knife to put it through my father's heart when he started to shout for help. The burglar then left, taking a watch and my parents' wallets with not more than twenty dollars in *baht*, plus my mother's silver party shoes, while she lay frozen with fear on the other twin bed.

The burglar, who was later apprehended, said that his religion prevented him from killing insects, reptiles, birds, animals, children, and women, and that he didn't approve of killing men, but my father had been noisy and so there was no choice. I was sound asleep in the next room and I knew nothing until next morning, by which time my mother had got help from the Embassy and from the police. She told me something equivocal, like "Daddy's had an accident, don't ask questions," and sent me to stay with the family of the Deputy Chief of Mission. I heard what really happened, with lots of blood included, from the servants there. By the time I rejoined my mother, the packers were in our house and very soon we flew to America, my home where I had never lived.

Not then or ever did my mother and I talk about the murder. Her alternating tears and stony despair dismayed me utterly. I felt guilty for my inability to console her, and more guilt about having failed my father as well. Why had I not heard the burglar and warned him? Why had I been such a boring child that he had always preferred his newspapers to me? The possibility that I, too, needed consoling, seems not to have occurred to either my mother or me.

Most of the people she knew lived in Washington, but she would not consider settling there. Without her husband, she knew she would feel like an outsider, and that if she were invited to a dinner party at all, she would be squeezed in where the nobodies always sat; never again would she be at a host's right. Washington is a company town, she used to tell me sadly. So we moved to New York, where she had a few friends who had nothing to do with the State Department. She sent me to boarding school in New England, and after that I went to Katharine Gibbs Secretarial School. There was not enough money for college, where I might possibly have developed my naturally studious mind and found a career beyond the typewriter.

Two of my Katharine Gibbs classmates asked me to join them in an apartment they had found, but when I broached the subject to my mother, she wept.

"You are too young."

"I'm nineteen. That's too *old* to be living with my mother."

"In my day, girls lived at home until they married."

"But this isn't your day."

She tried another tack. "You are young for your age. Foreign Service children often are. You know the capital of Swaziland, but you don't know how to cook, or mend your clothes. Who's going to tell you if your slip is showing? Who will do your laundry? Your hair will be a mess."

41

"I'll learn," I said angrily. "Other girls learn. Do you think there's something wrong with me?"

"Not wrong, just different. You weren't brought up like ordinary American girls. You are *different*."

"I don't want to be different," I said, and then I began to cry, too.

Finally we agreed to compromise. I would stay with her for another year. And she would stop babying me.

That same week, I was hired for a secretarial job at a new magazine called *Bystander*, where one of the four young men who owned it was named David Smithson.

Over the years, I have made it a rule not to think about David. But on that May afternoon following lunch with Lydia and Deck, I came home in a rage against him. After Oz returned to his office, I sat down on the swing on our *portal* and tried to settle my nerves by looking at my garden. I have found that thoughts of gardening can lift my spirits. The garden has its own world and nothing there talks back or asks me any questions, even the fat pale cricket called *niño de la tierra*, whose head is like a smiling child's face and looks as if it might have something to say. The flowers and shrubs inform me silently of their needs and I try to provide. This interchange seems to me more satisfactory than any of my human relationships, and more tranquilizing than Valium.

Fortunately, our *portal* faces away from the main house, so that Lydia can't see me "wasting time," which, it would appear, is a capital crime in Rhode Island. One time, when she caught me unoccupied, she called me over and put me to work stamping and sealing two hundred and fifty fundraising letters for the Animal Shelter.

In Santa Fe, anything will grow if you water it, and the flowers that were in bloom that day included the lavish opulent ones I love best: Emperor tulips, peonies, and huge purple lilacs, so big and billowy that the bushes hardly seemed able to hold them up. As I sat there, birds were singing snatches of inspired songs I never knew they knew. I thought, these birds are overachievers. Maybe they have even surprised themselves; especially the mockingbirds, with their bravura improvisations. The very small birds were making themselves look bigger by fluffing out the feathers on their heads. And the male house finches, whose heads and necks are a dull reddish gray most of the year, seemed to have put on scarlet hoods.

Cotton from the big cottonwoods by the arroyo was blowing like snow and floating into dark, rich places. Butterflies were darting, seeking, pollinating. A woodpecker, somewhere among the treetops, was knocking urgently on a hollow trunk. It was a sound like little hollow balls, bouncing fast, and it put me in mind of fast heartbeats.

I thought about David.

Listening to the woodpecker, I began to wonder when it was that my heart had first beat faster because of him, and it seemed to me that it may well have been the first time I ever saw him. He was striding around the halls of *Bystander*: late (he was always late), but when he got there he rushed around, stirring up action. To me, new there, and young—nineteen—he had movie-star good looks and charm, but, *like* a movie star, he was not (I thought) available to me and therefore not to be considered seriously. As we in the office all knew, he was unofficially engaged. Aside from that, I thought him inaccessible in other ways. His family name, unremarkable as it is, was one that my mother, when I told her, recognized at once. One of my mother's hobbies was knowing who was who.

"Smithson?" she said. "The Smithson Mills, in Rhode Island. A very old family. Was his grandfather called Osgood Decatur Smithson?"

"I don't know."

"Ask him."

"Oh, *no*, Mother."

I knew that she both longed for me to marry someone as exalted as David and was perfectly sure that I could never bring it off.

"It's a catastrophe that you have no father," she used to say. "I mean, an *established* father, like your poor Daddy would have been by now. It *places* a girl. If Daddy were alive today, everyone would place you: a State Department daughter. We'd be living overseas or in Washington and Daddy would be an ambassador. But as it is, no one knows anything about you. You are a nobody."

I was sure she was right, and that all that could ever happen between me and David would be that he'd chat with me by the watercooler. So I entertained no hopes whatsoever regarding him. It is a queer thing about love that the time when you first meet someone, and like him, and think he's extraordinarily nice but expect nothing, can be one of the happiest times.

David first asked me out to dinner late one hot summer afternoon, when, as he pointed out, sensible people were at the beach.

"Come on! Alex! Princess Alexandra! Let's go out tonight!" He made it sound so exciting. But I said no, because one did not go out with engaged people. I didn't want the others in the office talking about me or watching me for signs of a broken heart.

David's fiancée, Edwina Bishop, called Bishy, had been in the office a couple of weeks before, just before leaving to spend the summer in Europe with her family. David had introduced her all around, while they strolled from office to office, holding hands. On her third left finger was as large a diamond as I had ever seen. Now it is dull with dishwater and New Mexico dirt, but, of course, it is still big—three carats—and topples to one side of her slender finger.

On that bright summer day, Bishy wore a dress of crisp black linen, and a wide straw hat with a black ribbon. I made a mental note, then and there, that what basically sets the rich apart is that their clothes either are new or look like new because they are pressed. And I particularly envied Bishy her hat, even though I knew that had it been mine it would soon have been rained on or crushed in the subway crowds. (Conservative girls still wore hats then, although the days of general hatlessness were fast approaching.) My summer hat that year was a naive-looking straw bonnet from Bloomingdale's basement, which suited the look I was then unconsciously trying to project—that of a fragile young thing, deserving of protection and help. Now that I think back on it, I see that in that hat I suggested a somewhat demented shepherdess, wandering the streets of Manhattan in search of her sheep.

Bishy was wearing black patent leather pumps, and her long pretty legs were bare and very tan. Her face was more sweet than pretty. She had an habitual expression that seemed to say, if you tell me anything unpleasant I simply won't believe it. So keep telling me everything that is good news. Give me compliments. Take me to the theater. Buy me a white camellia and I'll pin it to the barrette in my sleek brown hair and then maybe I'll give you a wee sweet kiss.

I was certainly nothing at all like Bishy, so I was sure that if David liked her he wouldn't have the time of day for me. What I didn't realize was that David liked many different types of women. Practically all of them. There was plenty of room for me.

The second time David asked me out was after five on another hot and humid day. Most of the staff had gone home. He came charging into the alcove where I was typing.

"Let's go!"

"Where to?" I thought perhaps he had some letters to dictate, and I got out my notebook and pencil.

"Where to? To get a drink and have some dinner."

"Oh—I—" I was tongue-tied, but I managed to shake my head.

"Why not?" he demanded.

It seemed to me very silly to reply, "Because you're engaged." After all, he hadn't asked for my hand in marriage nor had he made an indecent proposal. He just wanted to have dinner.

So I said, "I've got on the wrong clothes." And I would have liked to add, "To go out to dinner with you I need a better haircut and a shower and a new dress, and actually I ought to have a different face and personality."

He understood some portion of that, and said, "Come on, you look fine. I like the way you look."

Walking along the street with him I saw myself in a mirror, and something made me like my looks, too. It was mostly because I looked happy. I took his arm when he offered it, crossing a busy street. Women don't do that much anymore, but it always seemed pleasant to me: a minor but subtle act of courtship. To touch without deliberate familiarity was one of the ways of raising the sexual temperatures of a man and a woman without anything needing to be said or commitments made.

We went to the Oak Room at the Plaza (where I had never been) and had drinks. I had a gin and tonic, and he had three. The 1912-ish mural over the bar, showing the Fifty-ninth Street Plaza as it once was, with carriages waiting in front of the hotel in a bluish twilight, spoke of mystery and sophistication. So did the other customers in the bar. Beautiful women, spectacularly well-dressed; and their escorts, who, like David, were superbly self-assured. And those who weren't handsome clearly felt that the way they looked was better than handsome.

Later we walked (in the bluish twilight of the mural) to the Italian Pavillion, that beautiful, long-gone restaurant on West Fifty-fifth Street. Having lived in Italy between the ages of eight and ten, I had the pleasure of translating the gigantic menu for David, glad to let him know I was not quite the simple little typist he may have taken me for. (As my mother would have said, I *placed* myself.) I also talked Italian with the waiter, finding out that he was a native of Tuscany, whereupon we exchanged expressions of rapture about the city of Florence. David was amused, and touched my hand. Then he asked me where else I had lived, and when I told him Uruguay, Turkey, Germany, Rhodesia, and Thailand, he said Good God, those places were a blank to him. Which one had I liked best?

"Rhodesia," I said, without hesitation.

"Yeah? Weren't you worried about the Mau Mau?"

"The Mau Mau were in Kenya, and anyway I was a kid and I didn't worry much." For an instant I saw my Shona nanny, playing tag with me in the garden of our Rhodesian house, in and out among mimosas and two-story-high poinsettias. "And that part of Africa is so beautiful," I added. "And surprising."

"Beautiful? Surprising? How about being more specific?"

"Well, there was a tree called a kaffirboom that all winter had no leaves but only very big red flowers, like something you might make out of crepe paper in kindergarten. And then, there was a

49

kind of worm, called a chungalolo. About a foot long, with a head at each end. He could go either way without turning around."

"Beautiful and surprising. Like you."

"Do I look like a two-headed worm?"

"No," he said, "No, you really don't, although I'm sure they're very nice." He took my hand. "I just think you're beautiful and surprising."

We took a taxi downtown to Eddie Condon's for a couple of hours lost in Dixieland jazz. At some point I called my mother and told her I would be late and not to wait up. Although I was grown up and earning my living, she nevertheless said, "I want you home by midnight. And be sure the young man brings you to the door and waits until you're up all three flights."

We lived in a walk-up on East Eighty-ninth Street, and my mother was ceaselessly on guard against burglars. I couldn't complain, in view of what had happened in Bangkok, but at that time, there were surely not nearly as many burglars in New York as she imagined, and I was tired of hearing about them.

Her voice on the telephone sounded very displeased, as if I had no business to be out on the streets unless she had planned it.

"Who, might I ask, invited you on such short notice?"

"David Smithson."

"That young man in your office? I thought you told me he was engaged."

"Mother, somebody is waiting for this phone booth. I have to go now," I said, and did so.

That brief telephone conversation stirred up the anxiety my mother and I shared: how was I ever going to perform the one most important task of a woman's life—to find and hang on to the right man? The dread alternative was to become a "career girl"; and, according to my training, career girls, such as Consulate or Embassy secretaries and the occasional female Foreign Service Officer, were objects of pity and scorn. My role models were State Department wives—serene, gracious, husband-enhancing. Some were beautiful and had acquired handsome husbands; some were plain and had plain husbands. The corollary between female beauty and handsome husbands seemed close—so that a girl like me, who was at best pretty but nowhere near beautiful, could not expect anyone much to look at. Nevertheless, many people much plainer than I had found some sort of husband; and even ugly couples, if they were friendly and hard-working, had been known to attain ambassadorial rank, or its equivalent in the outside world. So, my mother and I kept telling ourselves, I would most likely find Mr. Right or Mr. Quasi-Right; or rather, *he* would find *me*.

In my eagerness, I tried to please everyone, to

be whatever the young man at hand wanted me to be. I was glad to see any man who paid me attention; sorry when he left, worried when he didn't call. I was ready to like anything he liked, whether it was beer, the study of calculus, Richard Nixon, or the Rockette shows at Radio City. I had no native interest in sports, but I went along to football games in the foulest weather, standing up to cheer when my escort did, wondering why.

My mother didn't think much of any of the "boys" I went out with, most of whom I met through my classmates at Katharine Gibbs. She couldn't *place* them. So I began to have two sides to my life: one in which I was my mother's faithful little girl, and the other in which I associated with people who barely knew where Uruguay or Thailand were or that America had representatives in those places. The one I liked best, Walter N. Hofer, was big and overweight and never had clothes that fitted him. His red wrists and hands seemed to be escaping from his coat sleeves and his Adam's apple bobbed above a tight shirt collar. But I found him sweet, attentive, and interested in sexual dalliance of an unalarming kind. What I enjoyed most about him was what we then called necking, and since he had no car, this took place sitting on the stairs that led up to our third-floor walk-up. He was a student at NYU, the first college man in his family, and he intended to become a certified public accountant. I don't remember that we ever talked of marriage or even of going steady. I realized that Wally had a long way to go before he could afford to "get serious" and that was fine with me.

My mother was appalled by Wally, and said we'd better move to Washington so that I could look for a Foreign Service Officer. My sister had been successful in that maneuver, five years previously, and was now the wife of one of our Assistant Economic Officers in Munich.

"But I don't want a Foreign Service Officer, Mother," I said.

"Not want a Foreign Service Officer? Not want a man like Daddy?" And tears came into her eyes and her nose got red. I hated to have that happen. One couldn't urge her to stop mourning for her husband, and I always felt in despair of cheering her up. Nor could I explain that I didn't want to take to the road again, and the high seas, and the airplane journeys. I wanted to settle down for good and belong somewhere.

"Mother, half of New York is male," I pointed out. "Sooner or later, surely, one or two males will show up who are possibilities."

"But you won't be nice to them. You're only nice to undesirable NYU boys."

I did not suggest the possibility that I might never marry, because such a notion made me very anxious. Equally with my mother, I cherished the tale of the Sleeping Beauty, and had done so ever since my fourth birthday, when I was given *The Sleeping Beauty*, illustrated in silhouettes by Arthur Rackham. I had been instantly fascinated by Rackham's ominous fairyland: the stark, black, twisted trees, the bramble thickets, the bats, the spiney castle turrets, and the hunchbacked Bad Fairy. And I liked hearing the story over and over, of how a lovely princess, through no fault or action on her part, became enchanted and fell sound asleep for a hundred years, along with everyone else in her castle. The king fell asleep on his throne, the housemaids keeled over, brooms in hand, and the cooks stopped turning the spit and collapsed on the kitchen floor. There were no cobwebs because the spiders were asleep, but the castle became very dusty. At last, a prince fought his way to the castle gate through a hundred years of thorny undergrowth. He stepped over the sleeping guardsmen and bounded up the dusty stairs. In a tower bedroom, on a bed whose canopy had fallen into tatters, he found the princess—dusty, too, but as lovely as ever. He planted a kiss on her lips. And at once she jumped up, well-rested and ready to snap up the prince's proposal of marriage.

Now that I have become somewhat enlightened—through age and a few analytical insights—I realize that, for me, this was no ordinary fairy tale. *The Sleeping Beauty* exemplified the precepts that my mother had conscientiously passed on to me from her own early twentieth-century upbringing. Like the princess, a woman must be passive, a little dumb, and ready to be led; sweet at all times, uncomplaining when ill luck strikes. If she observes these simple rules, she will surely attract a prince—or, at least, some viable sort of husband. Otherwise, she will become one of life's discards, an old maid career girl.

By the time I had taken all these ideas in, they were already out of date. My sister Ginevra's daughter, born in the 1960s, never liked *The Sleeping Beauty*. Among fairy tales, she preferred *The Bremen Town Musicians*, with its nonstop action and its unisex, self-asserting characters.

Once, soon after I started at Katharine Gibbs, I thought I had hold of the Prince, in a young man I met at a party, Franklin Brock. He was from the Middle West, his father owned an enormous company that made pots and pans, and he drove a Cadillac convertible. It was summer when we met and he invited me to drive to Easthampton for the day, where we joined friends of his at the Maidstone Club. I felt at once that I registered as totally from away, because my bathing suit was neither new nor pressed and my skin was not tan. The other girls had skins like that of beautiful mulattoes, and their slender brown feet were adorned with exquisitely painted toenails. Mine were plain.

In the surf I got knocked down by waves. One of my breasts escaped from my bathing suit top, for the whole beach to see. This was not my fault, emphatically not my plan, but Franklin Brock was horrified as he pulled me to my feet and stood between me and the beach, not knowing what to say—doing nothing—certainly not touching it. I glanced down and covered it up. But I had lost Franklin.

"Why doesn't that nice Franklin call?" my mother asked, a day or two later.

"He's not going to."

"You've lost him?" she cried. "What did you *do*, Alexandra?"

Of course, I didn't tell her. She would have commanded that I stay away from beaches.

III

III

That first evening with David, I was convinced that there would be no sexual advances or even hints, because he was engaged to adorable Bishy. If, by remote chance, the subject should arise, I planned to act as if I had no idea of what he might be talking about. However, when he took me home, there was not even a kiss goodnight. The absent Bishy was probably on both our minds.

The following week, David was back at my desk.

"Let's go dancing tonight!"

Of course I wanted to go and of course I wanted to please him, but, again, I didn't like the way I looked.

"I've got on this old dress," I said dejectedly.

"Don't be silly. We'll go to the Village Vanguard and you'll be the prettiest girl they ever saw."

As it turned out, the dancing went so well that I forgot everything but what fun it was. I remembered hearing from my father about a musical comedy star of 1918 or so, Eva Tanguay, who threw herself about on the stage, singing a song called "I Don't Care"—with abandon, my father had said disapprovingly. Abandon was what I felt, dancing that evening.

In the taxi there was a lot of kissing. Next day David asked if I would have dinner with him on the following Monday.

"Get dressed up," he said. "We'll go to a really good restaurant. How about Twenty-One?"

I had read that name in gossip columns, but had never expected to set foot there. I spent all day Saturday shopping and put out three weeks' salary on an impractical, beautiful dress of the very palest pink silk, a color sometimes called ashes-of-roses, which suited my pale blond hair. I told my mother I was going to a party given by a female friend at *Bystander*; that she lived on the Upper West Side and that I would very likely spend the night with her if the party was a late one.

"What is her telephone number?"

"She doesn't have a phone."

"But, Alex, I need to know where you are. Suppose something happens to you?"

"Call the police."

David lived with a friend in the East Sixties, but after dinner that night, he explained that we weren't going there. Bishy, he said, sometimes telephoned him from Europe.

"She says she can't sleep," he said, "but she's just checking up on me."

"But you *are* engaged, aren't you?" I dared to say.

"Not seriously."

"But you gave her a ring."

"That was my mother's ring and my mother's idea. She and Bish try to tie me down, but they can't. I'm free, sweetheart." And he kissed me.

Like many another silly girl, I imagined that if a man wanted me, it was only me he wanted.

David took me to an incredibly dreary cold-water flat in the East Village, borrowed from one of the more raffish members of the *Bystander* staff, who kept it as a lovenest. I hated it. The stale air smelled of mice, and of long-ago meals of cabbage, and of more recent sweat. The kitchen counter, covered in stained oilcloth, was a staging area for cockroaches, even though there was nothing to eat there, only bottles of gin and bourbon. When we lay down on a dingy sofa bed, I saw a mouse zipping across the floor, and at that point I threw my arms around David's neck and confided that this was all fairly new to me.

"You mean—you're a *virgin*?" he asked.

I was so afraid of displeasing him that I said in a very low voice, "Sort of."

That made him laugh. Then he embraced me and said that was all right, that we'd sort of make love,

61

but that I could have the day off tomorrow if I'd go and see a doctor and "get fixed up."

"I'll probably have to wait for an appointment," I said. "Maybe weeks."

"Go to the emergency room."

Next day I managed to find a gynecologist and a prescription for the Pill. After that, the double life I led became even more complicated. It was hard to conceal anything from my mother in our small apartment, and I decided to keep my reserve pills in the hatbox that held her 1940s hats, feathered and veiled, which she had worn to receptions when we were in the Foreign Service. I knew she wouldn't look inside that box, because the sight of the hats made her cry. But neither would she throw the box away. Being a pleaser, it seemed vital to please my mother, and to her I tried to present an image of a chastity as guarded and hard to breach as the dikes of Holland. A white dress could scarcely be white enough for me on that mythical wedding day when she would watch me coming down the aisle.

Yet that summer, from June to September, David and I were intensely involved in sex, and I, at least, was in love. We were only four years apart in age, but David seemed about twenty years more experienced. He knew how to make me feel not only lusted for, but cherished. And that was of immense importance to me. In some deep sense, it was like finding a home at last. I felt surrounded, buoyed up by love, as surf surrounds you when you leave the beach: surrounds you, envelops you, makes a place for you.

All through the very hot summer, several nights a week, I found that home in David. Then, the rest of the evenings, I was "home" in the Eighty-ninth Street apartment with my mother. David always left on Thursdays to spend weekends with one of his partners on Long Island, taking work with him—which may have been one of the many reasons why *Bystander* did not succeed.

David and his partners had plunged into the New York publishing world with the arrogance of privileged children. I believed that their very arrogance carried them a long way—as a fast, shallow dive will carry a swimmer halfway across the pool. Probably because of his southwestern upbringing, David was not as conventional as his Harvard cronies—even though he belonged to the best Harvard clubs and admired Harvard traditions. He had drawn cartoons for the *Lampoon* and since graduating he'd received nice rejection letters from *The New Yorker*. Cartooning was probably the thing he did best, but he didn't regard it as a serious career, because he wasn't *that* unconventional. The small component of rebellion in David's nature (and which I had some of, too—one reason why we found each other so attractive) led him to try things he had not really thought over in depth. At twenty-one he had come into a million dollars. Invest it in a new magazine? Why not?

I think of him now, coming to work at eleven in the morning, full of the excitement of new plans and complicated schemes. Sometimes when his face was in repose—waiting for an elevator, perhaps—his youth, his twenty-three years, suddenly became very obvious. He looked puzzled, even anxious. But not for long. Someone would speak to him and immediately he would become animated and full of wit. There was always a lot of laughing wherever he was. I can't document what was actually said, and nothing dates as fast as a style of humor. Even if I could remember the funny things he said in the Sixties, they probably wouldn't seem so funny now.

His good looks, though, were timeless. He was six feet tall, black-haired and blue-eyed. I came to know how the pupils of those blue eyes became larger and darker in dim light, reminding me of the dark sapphire of midocean.

He was not an intellectual, but his mind retained all kinds of information with the ease of a computer, and he could talk superficially about almost anything. Sometimes he went on at length about sports (where he completely lost me) or about Dixieland jazz and its musicians (where I learned to follow him). Eddie Condon, Muggsie Spanier,

Wild Bill Russell, and the rest soon became famil-
iar to me. I knew what instruments they played
and where they were born and whose bands they
had formerly played in, just as David did. At his
side, at Condon's or the Village Vanguard, I heard
old songs and the words are still in my head:
"Georgia On My Mind," "Jada," "The Sheik of
Araby." We decided to pick "our song" and it
became "How High the Moon." The bittersweet-
ness of the words and the minor notes in it thrilled
and saddened me. David was too high a moon.

"You and I can't go out for a while," David told
me in September. "My mother and father are in
town. I'm trying to get a loan from my dad, so
I've got to be nice."

It seemed that his parents had come East for a
week's holiday, and that Bishy and her parents had
returned from Europe. The four older people were
good friends. Every evening all six had dinner
together and went to the theater or to a nightclub.
Then Bishy went back to Mount Holyoke for her
senior year, and David came back to me as if he
had never been away. I wondered if he had missed
me, even though he said he did. Had I missed
him? Without David, all days were rainy and all
lights were out.

In late November, I was stunned to read in the
Sunday *New York Times* the announcement of the

engagement of Miss Edwina Bishop of Brookline, Mass., to Mr. David Smithson, of Santa Fe, New Mexico. The following evening, Monday, David took me to dinner. Monday was our usual night. I began to cry in the restaurant and embarrassed him.

"Listen, *I* didn't put that announcement in the paper. The Bishops did. They didn't even ask me."

"Then tell them to print a retraction—that is, if it's not true."

"Well, that would be a little hard on Bishy, don't you think? Anyhow, she doesn't want to get married until she graduates from college and that won't be until next June. A lot can happen between now and then."

"Like what?"

We were side by side on a banquette, and he put his arm around me. "Don't worry, I'll think of something. But for heaven's sake, quit crying and eat your dinner."

Later we went to the East Village flat, and into the breakers that continued crashing so splendidly around our heads.

Just before Christmas, David gave me a round-trip ticket to Santa Fe, for over New Year's. It was his Christmas present, and the envelope was tied with a red ribbon and included also a little box containing a pair of pearl earrings from Tiffany. I was delighted with the earrings, but doubtful about the ticket. I wondered—as I still do—what he thought he was doing. Was it to make me stop crying? If so, he clearly hadn't thought the matter through. Introspection was not only foreign to his nature, he thought it was unmanly. He called it "contemplating your navel." So it was up to me to do the wondering and pondering, and to this day I am surprised that I accepted that trip to New Mexico when it should have been evident, even to my muddled head, that David and Bishy would sooner or later be married.

"Will she be there?" I demanded.

"Honestly, I don't think so," he said, "but I can't absolutely promise. My parents could get into the act and invite the whole Bishop family. But it's a house party, darling. Lots of people. So, come on, please be there. Be there because I want you!"

One thing about uncontemplative men like David, they usually say what they mean—or, at least, what they think they mean. Whether, in the toils of David's unconscious mind, he wanted two women vying for him, or whether he wanted to show his mother that he could pick his own girls without any help from her—or—or. But when he said "Be there because I want you," I couldn't resist that plea.

I flew to New Mexico on the last day of December. The sun was setting while we were over the plains of western Kansas, prompting the pilot to call our attention to the snowy peaks ahead, part of the southern Rocky Mountains. They were fiery red with the sunset. I felt as though I were entering a different and enchanted world. Later I found out that those words had been appropriated by the State of New Mexico Tourism Office. "Land of Enchantment" was the message on the license plates. Santa Fe was "The City Different." I wince at those words now. Nevertheless, they still bring to mind that December sunset and those peaks of fire and snow.

Then the moon rose, and, as we flew on, the terrain below became more hilly and the snowy ground was dotted all over with dark, roughly circular shapes. These were piñon and juniper trees. Later, when I came to know these trees at eye level, I saw how gnarled and sturdy they are, like very old people who are survivors and stayers. They are the essence of this ancient and uncompromising part of the world.

I looked eagerly for David the minute I got off the plane, but he wasn't there. Baffled and a little frightened, I waited by the baggage carousels, wondering what I should do after retrieving my suitcase. Then a tall, thin-faced young man came up and asked if I were Alexandra Burrows.

"How did you know?" I asked, much relieved.

"David told me to look for a pretty girl, looking dazed," he said. "in a—uh—fur coat. And, by the way, I'm David's brother. Oz."

Much later, Oz told me that David had said to look for a pretty girl, looking dazed, in a *funny-looking* fur coat. I was wearing my mother's twenty-year-old Australian opossum, and funny-looking was too kind a word for it. It was yellowed and shapeless and unrecognizable as any known kind of fur. Hedgehog, maybe.

"Where's David?" I asked.

"Ma needed him at home. Too many guests." Oz was looking the crowd over. "I'm supposed to pick up two more people I've never seen before. Friends of my parents, from Chicago."

After a while, we found both my suitcase and the Chicago couple, Mr. and Mrs. Furlong. From the airport, at Albuquerque, to the Gallegos Ranch is about seventy miles, mostly on the highway. I was too disappointed at not being met by David to do any talking. I sat silently beside Oz, and the Furlongs chattered away in the back seat.

Mr. Furlong said it was good to feel this dry cold air, so different from the humid cold of Lake Forest, where they lived; but just the same they were glad that their next destination was the Caribbean.

"We had no idea it would be cold here," Mrs. Furlong put in. "We were packing nothing but resort clothes. After all, we've been to Tucson and it's warm there."

Oz explained, "We are seven thousand feet high."

"It was certainly lucky for us that we called

Lydia to check about what to bring," Mr. Furlong said. He sounded annoyed, as if he had been deliberately deceived. It's an attitude I've often seen in visitors. They think Santa Fe is in Arizona and should have grapefruit orchards and giant cacti.

By the time we arrived at Gallegos Ranch it was after midnight and the rest of the house party had gone to bed. Oz found a note from Lydia, saying "Saving our strength for New Year's Eve. See you at breakfast." The Furlongs were billeted in the main house and I in the guesthouse (where Oz and I later lived). An aunt of Lydia's was occupying the big bedroom there, and I had a sliver of a room with Southwest furniture in it. Being ignorant of such things, I mistook it for junk. In fact, the narrow, uncomfortable Taos bed was a good antique, and the crooked chest of drawers had been made in some mountain village a hundred years before. On top of this chest was a hastily scribbled note from David: "Mother asked the Bishops. Thank God you're here!! Can't wait to see you. XXXXXXXXX D."

I went to bed, wearing my new pearl earrings, which seemed to make me feel less lonely.

Next morning I put on a sweater twin-set and a wool skirt. Surely that was correct for a morning in the country? No, it was not. The six or seven other young people I met in the dining room were all in ski pants and heavy hand-knit sweaters.

"Didn't you bring your skis?" someone asked me. "Would you like to borrow some?"

"I don't ski."

"Don't *ski*?" The girl looked at me curiously. "I thought maybe you'd hurt your leg or something."

I wished I'd thought of that very good excuse. Another of the girl guests was on crutches and was getting lots of attention and waiting-on.

Lydia Smithson came into the room. At that time she was in her fifties, an outstandingly handsome woman. With her quick gestures and long, narrow body, she might have been thought younger had it not been for her weather-beaten complexion. New Mexico is unkind to the faces of women, especially of those who ski, ride, and spend a lot of time outdoors. The deep furrows that now riddle Lydia's face had already started. They remind me of the furrows left by flash floods in this dry land.

She extended her long, thin hand to me. "Miss Burrows? How nice you could join us. But you don't ski, I understand. Never mind. We have horses. And a skating pond."

My heart sank. I had never learned to do anything well in the way of sports.

"I like walking," I dishonestly said. "I really *love* to walk."

"Splendid. We'll send you out to exercise the dogs."

This was my first encounter with Lydia Smithson and it was remarkably predictive of how our relationship would develop. I knew she was forming an unfavorable opinion of my degree of self-possession. On my part, I was sizing her up as malevolent.

"David and his fiancée left early," she went on, "to get a full day of skiing at Taos. David's asked Osgood to look after you today, but he is not up yet."

"Osgood?"

"Our older son."

"Oh," I said. "I thought you called him Oz."

"We do," she said.

I thought, she is going out of her way to leave me out of the "we." She wants to tell me that there are insiders and outsiders. And yet how could she possibly do anything that silly? Over the years I found out: she could.

The rest of the skiers left the house soon after. Osgood Decatur Smithson IV appeared about half an hour later, and we seemed to be the only ones left in the house.

"I'm afraid I'm keeping you from skiing," I said. "Please don't stay home on my account. Your mother told me to walk the dogs." Actually I was afraid I was going to cry, and for that reason wouldn't have minded being alone. I was only half aware of what I was saying to Oz, making idiot pleasantries just as I had often seen my parents do over the years. I wasn't bad at that.

Oz didn't have much small talk, but he had the grace to appear interested in my chatter. He said, "I really would like to show you around. Do you want to see some Indian ruins? Los Alamos? Eat some chili?"

"All of it," I said, and my mother would have been proud of my enthusiasm and warmth.

All morning, Oz drove me along winding two-lane roads in the brilliant sunshine and the cold clear air. The sky was as blue as a sky can get—bluer than it ever gets over Santa Fe nowadays, because of automobile exhausts and jet trails. The barren landscape offered subdued colors: pink rocks, gray cottonwood trunks, dark red branches of salt cedar, pale yellow dirt of dry arroyos. Here in the valley, no snow was on the ground. For snow, you had to raise your eyes to the slopes of the mountains. Houses were few. You could look in many directions and see none, or one. Terrain like this seemed to me overwhelming—more like the bottom of the ocean, minus the water, than a place to live. And I was already overwhelmed in another way—by David's carelessness. Why had he brought me all this way, knowing that I couldn't ski or ride or fit in at all? Or had he not been listening when I had tried to make this clear? And I *had* tried, more than once. I had told him about beginning to ski when we were stationed in Germany, and then, just as I was catching on, finding myself in Bangkok, fourteen degrees from the equator. The idea occurred to me that my feelings and concerns were of less than urgent interest to him.

Had it not been for David forsaking me, I would have enjoyed this day with his brother. We stopped for lunch at the Rio Grande Cafe, in Espanola, where I ate my first enchilada and did not blink or choke over the hot green chili.

Oz expressed surprise and I explained, "It's because I used to live in Bangkok—" which surprised him even more. When I recited the other places where I'd lived, he asked me where home was (not "what place did you like best?", which most people asked). I said, "Nowhere." But then he looked so concerned and sorry for me that I added, "I don't mind."

"Maybe I envy you," he said after a pause. "New Mexico is my home, but, you know, none of us Anglos can ever feel completely natural here. There's always something a little exotic about it, a little bit stagey. It really belongs to the Indians and the Spanish."

Then he started telling me about his horse. I could see that fear of introspection must be a Smithson family trait. He was voluble on the subject of his horse, of which he was very fond, and his short-haired German pointers. He said he did a lot of hunting. I tried to find out from him just what it was he liked about depriving wild things of their lives, but one seldom gets answers from hunters. Since then it has occurred to me that one reason he hunts is because his mother is so violently opposed to it. This is one way he can assert himself against her. But if that's so, I am sure he is unaware of it.

Oz and I spent the afternoon making *farolitos* for the party. A *farolito* is a new brown paper bag, filled with enough sand to hold a candle upright in it. Eighty or more, spaced evenly along the driveway and by the front door and on the roof give a festive, glowing light to welcome the party guests.

I found I was enjoying myself—or, at least, more than I would have thought possible. Oz was nice. Not as handsome as David, not as bright, not as funny. But, I thought, better endowed with common sense.

When I got back to the guesthouse, Lydia's aunt, my housemate, was looking for me. She wanted to propose that I bathe and dress for the party first as she'd like to take her time and was in no hurry. She was a woman in her seventies, pretty and chatty. She sat down on a corner of my bed and told me several things that depressed me, such as that Bishy was a lovely girl and the Bishops were just about the dearest people in the world; that they were so happy to be getting David as a son-in-law because he was such a steady young man and they knew he would take good care of their darling. And David had started a wonderful magazine that everyone in the East expected would put *The New Yorker* out of business. And how nice it was that I had been able to come, and where had I known Oz before? Oz was—well—different from David, but he was very nice, too. Quiet. Not so ambitious. Not such a live wire. But awfully nice.

I put on my evening dress. It was very conventional —dark blue velvet, strapless, with a full skirt. With David's pearl earrings and a pearl necklace borrowed from my mother, I thought I looked appropriate. My mother would have said so. But when I went to the main house, I found that the other girls were wearing Mexican or Indian clothes: bright, swirling skirts, off-the-shoulder blouses, concho belts, long clanky earrings, and armloads of silver bracelets.

Girls can be merciless when it comes to judging the clothes of other girls. I felt their glances, which said, "Who in the world can *this* be?" But the situation was alleviated by the arrival of David, who ran to me with a cowboy whoop and seized me in his arms.

"Queen Alexandra, sweetheart, am I glad to see *you!*"

I smiled as best I could, but he saw that I was at

the point of weeping. He shepherded me into the library and closed the door.

"Alex, come on, don't be mad at me. I can't help it that the Bishops are here. Ma did it. Did Oz treat you right today?"

"Of course. He's very nice. But did you ask me here so Oz could show me around?"

"Don't be silly. Things just got screwed up. Listen, you look terrific. Never saw a prettier girl."

"Why didn't you tell me that I was supposed to look Mexican? I feel really dumb."

He let go of me and began pacing the room. I could see that I'd better stop complaining; it would get me nowhere, except lower in his estimation. I found a mirror to peer into and wiped away the tears. Then I smiled at David.

He said, "Sorry, sorry, sorry. I really am, baby. I wanted you to have a good time here."

"I will," I said. "I am already." I was always afraid, when he was anything but his most cheerful self, that he might stop loving me, or that he had already. I added, "When does the music start?"

"When you and I start it." He looked happy again.

A mariachi band would begin later, but right now there was plenty of recorded music, at a deafening pitch, and colored lights flashing on the dance floor (which was the *sala* with all the furniture removed). David and I were first. I saw Bishy on the sidelines, scowling, but David seemed not to notice her. There was no doubt that we two danced well, and after that I got a succession of partners. One of them was Oz, with a smooth, respectable, coming-out-party style of the Fifties, which was when he had learned to dance. Later on, Mr. Smithson cut in and turned out to dance better than anyone there. Both he and Oz foundered when rock-and-roll was played, but I acquired other partners, whose names I never discovered. I had to admit to myself that I was having a good time.

As midnight approached, I looked around for David, but he was nowhere in sight. Neither was Bishy. Some of the guests had gone out to skate on the little pond, and I supposed that was where the two of them were. So, I thought, he can't be bothered, even at midnight—. But the sentence wouldn't finish itself. Clearly there was no way to deal with David except on his own terms.

I decided to go back to the guesthouse, perhaps to freshen up and then return, perhaps to go to bed and be miserable. I hadn't decided. On the way, I saw a man and a girl running on the frozen, moonlit lawn, laughing and falling down. I recognized David's enthusiastic laughter. Then he picked up the girl in his arms—she was Bishy, of course—and spun her around and around.

"Happy New Year, Happy New Year," he kept shouting. I could tell that he was half drunk; maybe two thirds. "Happy, happy, happy—"

Bishy said, much more calmly, "David, this time next year, we'll be married."

He set her down and began waltzing with her, singing inexplicably, "Boys and girls together/ Me and Mamie O'Rourke/ We'll trip the light fantastic/ On the sidewalks of New York."

I wondered whether Bishy found him as hard to understand as I did. If I had continued walking across the lawn, they would have seen me, so I went back to where the music was and danced some more. I felt like someone in a Hieronymus Bosch painting, dancing crazily while the Plague, or Death, or Devils struck down other dancers and hauled them away to a realm of skeletons and batfaced monsters. It would be only a matter of time before they got to me.

In a little while, David came to find me. I was dancing with his father, and he cut in.

"Come here," he said, whirling me into a corner, where he gave me a long, slow kiss. "Damn, where have you been? I've been looking for you."

Although I knew that wasn't true, I couldn't help putting my arms around his neck and kissing him back.

"I wish we were alone," he said in my ear. "Sweetheart, my darling, I really feel terrible—that I can't be with you every minute."

I could lie, too. "I'm having a terrific time," I said. Just then his father came and reclaimed me, and somehow I didn't see David again for the rest of the night.

Since I had to be in Albuquerque before noon on New Year's Day to catch my plane back to New York, I set the alarm for seven. But I was awake before it went off, and then, trained as I was never to miss transportation, I dressed and was ready to leave within fifteen minutes. A wintry sunrise was just taking place behind the eastern mountains, and when I looked out of the window I saw no life except for a jackrabbit, as big as a dachshund, loping over the frozen lawn. Snores came from Lydia's relative in the next room. I decided that I might venture into the main-house kitchen and perhaps find some instant coffee and a bite to eat, without fear of having to make conversation with anyone.

But when I opened the kitchen door I was greeted by sounds of chopping. Bishy stood at a butcher block table, wielding a knife over vegetables. We said hello, and, perhaps because these greetings were so lacking in warmth, I added, "Happy New Year."

"Happy New Year. You're up early," Bishy said, scooping up a pile of chopped carrots and throwing them into a pot.

"So are you," I said. "What are you making?"

"Soup. Soup for Auntie Lydia. I thought it was the least I could do, since she's been so wonderful to us all. And I've been taking cooking lessons."

"Good for you," I said. "I'd offer to help but I have to catch a plane."

"So soon?"

"Yes," I said. "So soon." I looked around desperately for something to eat—anything—so that I could get out of there. Bishy had put down her knife and was pulling up a chair for me. I was sorry to note that she looked fresh and blooming, with no sign of having overdone New Year's Eve. Her abundant satiny brown hair was brushed and tied back with a ribbon, her face was scrubbed, and under a businesslike chef's apron she wore a neat gray sweater and skirt. Indeed, she might have been waiting to be photographed for an article on New Year's cooking. I was glad that at least she hadn't seen my frowsy hedgehog coat.

"May I pour you a cup of hot coffee?" she inquired, very polite.

Automatically imitating my mother, I said, "Oh, I'd *love* it, how *nice* of you, Bishy!"

"Would you like a bowl of cornflakes?"

"Perfect."

Bishy set the breakfast in front of me and then sat down. I began to realize that there was more on her mind than an exhibition of good manners.

"How long have you known David?" she asked.

"David? Oh, I guess since last summer."

"I was wondering how come he invited you here."

I was thrown off base. My mother's manners were not going to help now. I met her cold gaze and realized that she intended an inquisition.

"Maybe you should ask him," I said.

"I did. He said you work in the office and you'd never been West. He made it sound as though he was sorry for you."

I didn't like that much, but I tried not to show it.

"Okay," I said. "So he's sorry for me."

"Do you agree with that?"

"Bishy," I burst out, "what's the point you're trying to make?"

"That David and I are engaged. I'm wondering whether that is entirely clear to you."

Before I could get together an answer, she went on, "I thought you were supposed to be some poor little typist that David was being kind to. But you don't act like it. All that dancing and cavorting around last night, and that great big revolting kiss you gave him. None of that looked much like a poor little typist to *me*. So I thought I'd better tell you something, now that I have the chance. Leave him alone. He's not yours. And it wouldn't be *good* for him right now to have you chasing after him."

I rose to my feet. "Now I'll tell *you* something," I said. "I think you are boring and arrogant and you don't know what you are talking about." Then, leaving the coffee and cereal untouched, I left the kitchen.

Crossing the lawn, I ran into Oz, who was supposed to drive me to the plane and had been to the guesthouse to make sure I was up.

"There's plenty of time before we have to leave," he said. "I could make breakfast for you."

"No thanks," I said. "Let's leave now. Right now."

"Right now? I'd better wake David. He wanted to be sure to say good-bye."

"You say good-bye for me. Just say I said thanks a lot."

In mid-January, the staff of *Bystander* got termination notices. No more magazine. I found a secretarial job at the *Ladies' Home Journal*, and David went home to New Mexico—to lick his wounds, he said.

"I have to recover from this mess at *Bystander*," he told me, the last time we visited the cold-water flat. "I probably won't be writing or calling—but I know you'll understand."

One day in March I got a telephone call from Oz. He was in New York—on vacation, he said—and David had given him my telephone number. He wanted to know if I'd like to see a musical with him. Later I learned that his purpose in coming to New York was to see me. Indeed (he said) to see me *a lot*. I was flattered and amazed, and, also concerned about what David might have told him about me. But it was soon clear that David had said very little.

"When I asked for your phone number," Oz said, "he was surprised and maybe not too pleased. I think he likes you pretty much himself."

"Do you mind?" I asked quickly.

"He's always been a dog in the manger," Oz said.

"David and I used to be really fond of each other," I said. I thought I needed to warn him a little, and he seemed to understand that.

"But this time he can't get in my way. He's engaged and the wedding's all planned for June."

"Oh."

"So what shows would you like to see?"

"I don't care," I said; for at that moment I cared about nothing except the appalling news I had just heard.

We went out nearly every evening for two weeks, and from morning till night on the weekends. ("He's giving you a *rush*," purred my mother.) We saw nine shows, ate ethnic meals all over town, and admired countless sights, including some I had never been to, such as the Brooklyn Museum and the Statue of Liberty. Toward the end of his stay, I took a day off from work in order to help him sightsee. Without making any amatory advances beyond a kiss or two goodnight, he told me that he had fallen in love with me and would I please think about marrying him.

My mother was ecstatic. Here he was at last, the prince himself, loaded with the proper credentials; and what was the Sleeping Beauty going to do about it? Just lie there?

I had a strong desire to telephone David, if only

to let him know what was going on. But common sense prevented me. After all, I knew he wouldn't say the only thing I wanted to hear, which was "Don't marry Oz, marry *me*."

The evening before Oz left town, he wanted to know if I had decided anything. It crossed my mind to tell him about David and myself, but, after all, that was in the past now, and Oz was not easy to communicate with on a personal level. If David chose to tell him later, then I would deal with it later.

What I said was, "I like you, I like you very, very much, but love? I can't honestly say that I love you."

"You'll get to," Oz said. "I'm not worried."

"Well, then, I won't worry either," I said.

We let my mother send an engagement announcement to *The New York Times*, in which Oz's connections and ancestry took up most of the space. Not long after that, I think, the *Times* gave up including centuries-old family data in these notices, but at that time they were still willing to write, "Mr. Smithson is descended from four colonial governors of Massachusetts, and from the noted eighteenth-century shipowner Silas Smithson. . . . Miss Burrows' late father, Fielding Burrows, was a Foreign Service Officer."

In June, Oz insisted that I accompany him to the Bishop-Smithson wedding in Brookline, at which

Oz was his brother's best man. I need not have dreaded it: there were about five hundred people present, and I barely caught a glimpse of the happy pair. The only time I was even close to David was when the rice was being thrown and he and Bishy, dressed for travel, were running out the big front door of the Country Club, making for a car that had "Just Married" scrawled in soap on the back window. David seemed bewildered. He stared at the cheerful faces and the raised arms, throwing rice, as if he feared these people and what they were doing. As he turned to get into the driver's seat, a particularly large handful of rice spattered over his back. He looked back, frowning, and at that moment saw me. I think it was distress I saw on his face, and I wished I could say, "I didn't do this to you, David. You did it to yourself."

He took the driver's seat, while his bride ran around to the other door and jumped in beside him. In no time they were down the drive and gone. Only Bishy waved.

+ IV +

After the Bishop-Smithson wedding, Oz kept after me to set our date. So did my mother. But I told them both, as crossly as I knew how, that I had suddenly become very interested in my *Ladies' Home Journal* job and would like to go on working for a while. There were unmarried "career girls" there of all ages, who loved their work and made good money and didn't seem to feel at all like despised old maids.

In July my mother had a stroke. I felt guilty, even though common sense told me that I hadn't caused it, or that even if I had, a stroke was an unfair weapon for a mother to use. But when I saw her lying in her hospital bed with one side of her mouth drawn up and her eyes full of anxiety, I leaned close to her and said, "Please stop worrying. I'm going to marry Oz."

I knew she wanted to ask "When?", so I added, "Soon. Just as soon as you get better."

She stirred, and then, quite distinctly in view of the fact that she had not said a word since the stroke, she whispered, "Say. Say name."

I understood and answered, "Mrs. Osgood Decatur Smithson Fourth."

My mother died a few hours later, looking very peaceful.

By overseas telephone to Munich, I discussed plans with my sister Ginevra. She said she couldn't leave her husband and small children, and we decided that I had better quit my job and take care of everything that had to be done. It was only a year since the summer of meeting David, but I felt infinitely older now, although, in fact, I was only twenty. Every day there were decisions to make, having to do with the dismantling of the apartment. I tried to follow the rule "Keep nothing that you do not know to be useful or believe to be beautiful," but another category, "Sentimental value," kept getting in the way. So I kept twenty-four black-and-gold lacquer finger bowls from Thailand, and an Italian pearwood desk, pretty but collapsing, and platters and trays suitable for serving hors d'oeuvres to a hundred people, all because they brought back memories of my perigrinating childhood. Never mind that I had not enjoyed my childhood much; these objects took the place of roots. There were at least a dozen framed photographs showing Consul and Mrs. Burrows in action: shaking hands with VIPs from Washington (John Foster Dulles, William Fulbright, Harold Stassen) and famous others (Adlai Stevenson, Louis Armstrong, Paul Tillich), plus noncelebrities, such as a girls' choir from Ohio; and one poignant photograph in a silver frame, showing Fielding and Alice Burrows—she in one of her beloved veiled hats—in Rhodesia, proudly on their way to a reception for some visiting British royalty.

One late afternoon, as I was sitting on the floor of the apartment living room, surrounded by photograph albums and loose snapshots, the telephone rang and it was David. He was in New York, he'd heard from Oz that I was there, and how would I like to be taken out for dinner? I said yes, without beating around the bush. After I had hung up I realized that I was making a serious mistake. Dread crept into me and made me cold, and my fingers trembled as I changed my clothes. I knew that it was a mistake to see David, and that if anything to be sorry about happened, I was walking into it idiotically, with my eyes wide open. I told myself severely to be sure to say goodnight right after dinner and come home alone.

We had one of our dinner and dancing evenings, exactly like the ones of the summer before. Except this time neither of us talked much, and I couldn't even tell whether he was enjoying himself or was sorry he'd suggested this. Once, as he took me in his arms on the dance floor, he said, "Your hand is cold." I said, "I know." And, I thought, it is cold with fear.

When he brought me home, he came up the three flights without asking, or being asked. And as soon as the door was closed behind us in the apartment, we began to make love. Then I knew why I was with him at all this evening. I was obsessed. There was no other way to explain it. Here was a man at the mercy of strong but capricious feelings whose very existence he could not face or deal with. Common sense should have told me that such a man was dangerous for me. But I had no common sense.

I thought of the story of Adèle, the daughter of Victor Hugo, which I remembered reading somewhere. Abandoned by her lover, an English army officer, she pursued him to his post in Canada, followed him everywhere, and spied upon him as he trysted with other women. She was crazy with love. In the end, she was restored to her family in France and lived to be an old woman, permanently mad. Although I had never tried to pursue David, I knew exactly how Adèle Hugo must have felt. The poor girl's love had little or nothing to do with the virtues of her beloved. It was simply that with him she had met love itself. She had met Eros. She had found that place where she wanted to be, and there could be no turning back.

I began to understand certain Greek myths, which I had once thought of as tedious. I had always thought it implausible that Aphrodite, the beautiful goddess who arrived from the sea on a fragile scallop shell (I pictured her as the Botticelli maiden, with her long yellow hair blowing and her eyes full of mysteries) could be the same woman who later proved so merciless and kept gods and humans in a continual state of turmoil. But now I was suddenly learning about the terrible contradictions of love.

David and I were together every night during the three weeks he was in New York. All reason disappeared. Judgment? Common sense? Discretion? I ignored them, and I never dared wonder, let alone ask, what David might be thinking or feeling. I knew he was in the city to look for a job, while Bishy was in Maine with her family, but I never questioned him. To ask might have led to finding out for sure what I believed to be true— that his feelings came and went as surprises to him, and when they went, he never attempted to detain them in order to find out more about them. Feelings, for David, were not a part of reality. He could not take them seriously. He understood the reality of a depleted bank account, and he knew that finding a job was a real necessity, but he did not understand the reality of feelings, and, except when making love, I think he was frightened of them.

One night he arrived at Eighty-ninth Street, very pleased with himself. He had found a job. With pride, as if speaking of a profession well-known for its prestige, he told me that he had been hired as a voice-over.

"That's terrific, David," I said, putting my arms around him. "What exactly is it?"

To illustrate, he made up a little scene for me. Standing in front of the open refrigerator, he pointed silently to the ice trays, the vegetable bin, the meat compartment. Then he went out of the room and I heard him saying in great excitement, "Why live in the past? Say good-bye to that out-of-date refrigerator. Time for Imperial, the refrigerator you've always wanted. Automatic defrost. Ice whenever you need it. Vegetables kept garden-fresh—" And more. Then he came back in, with a big smile. "That's a voice-over. You hear me but you don't see me."

"Do you think you'll like it?"

"It's hard, but if you catch on you can make money. I didn't think I could do it, at first, but they kept on training me because they like my voice."

"So do I," I said. And I could understand why the TV people liked it. It had exuberance and style, and was capable of suggesting sexiness even when the subject was refrigerators. The western and Harvard elements of his speech blended nicely, too, and gave him the sound of an American for all seasons.

David's part-time career as a voice-over began back then. And more than once I have been startled, not to mention shaken, to hear him speaking from my television set. The charm and enthusiasm and impression of sincerity that first attracted me to him have apparently had the same effect on the buying public. He sounds like Mr. American Everyman, a nice fellow eager to share a special treasure with you. Sometimes his commercials have been repeated for weeks, and they have brought him enough money to help keep the ranch solvent.

A few days later, David told me he was leaving for Maine to bring Bishy back to look for an apartment.

"When are you and Oz going to be married?" he asked.

I certainly did not want to talk about that. "I don't know," I said.

"I wish it were never," he said. "I wish—"

"What?"

He paused and then said, "I guess, that things were different."

I hoped he might say more, but he only added, "It's funny, all that's happened."

"*Not* funny," I said.

"Oh, I didn't mean funny-lots-of-laughs. Of course not. I'm talking about funny-strange."

I felt weary and impatient. There was only one thing I wanted to hear and that was that he loved me. But he only said it—and rarely—in those moments when ecstasy seemed to wrench it out of him.

"David," I said, "Please. Let's not have a long good-bye. Just go."

"Whatever you like," he said, and rose to leave. "But it won't be for long. I'll be back, sweetheart. Probably in a month or two and then I'll be living here in New York. Sit tight."

But I did not sit tight. I spent the next five weeks dismantling the vanished life of the Burrows family, and then I took a plane for Munich. My reason for going to Germany was not that I longed to see my sister, to whom I had never felt close, but that she was my only family and I needed emotional support. I was pregnant.

Whatever I decided to do about it, I didn't wish to consult David, even if I could have reached him. I would need to borrow money from Ginevra and pay it back when our mother's estate was settled.

Ginevra met me at the Munich airport. In an international crowd, my sister's Americanness was unmistakable. She was a tall, athletic young woman with a lot of well-brushed blond hair, the same shade as mine, only mine was curly and hers straight. Her friends called her Ginny, which was much better suited to her than the Florentine

Ginevra. Our parents had bestowed that name upon her because they had been vacationing in Florence about the time of her conception. The historical Ginevra was Ginevra dei Benci, daughter of a great Renaissance family. During a party to celebrate her betrothal, fifteen-year-old Ginevra had climbed into an empty chest while playing hide-and-seek. The lid banged down and she could not lift it again. She suffocated.

Our Ginevra would never have done such an unwise thing. She was capable and full of sense. Lost American tourists were likely to spot her in the streets of Munich and hurry over to ask directions to the opera house or to the Bayerischerhof Hotel; or they might even ask how much to tip a taxidriver and what a bratwurst is made of. Like our mother, Ginevra threw herself into her role of good State Department wife. After less than two years in Munich, her German was fluent and her two older children attended German schools and were often dressed in pint-size lederhosen or dirndls.

I had told her on the telephone only that I wanted to come for a short visit. The rest of the story was too hard to tell on the phone, and now, driving from the airport in Ginevra's new BMW, it seemed too hard to tell at all.

"Where's Osgood?" Ginevra began. "When's the wedding?"

"There won't be one."

"What?!" she exclaimed. "But in one of the last letters Mother wrote to me, she was so full of plans for it."

"She was *always* full of my wedding plans. And at the end, I told her it would happen. But now I'm not going to marry him."

"Oh, Alex! He sounds perfect. Rich, good-looking, Harvard—what more can you want?"

"It's my decision, after all," I said. "It's me he wanted to marry, not Mother. And I just didn't think he was right for me."

At a stop light, Ginevra turned and looked at me penetratingly.

"I think you're a little sad," she said, and reached out a sympathetic hand. "Is something the matter?"

"Yes," I said. "I'm pregnant."

The light changed and Ginevra very carefully shifted gears and got the car going again. Then she said, "And Osgood won't do anything?"

"It's not his."

"My God," she said. After that, I felt that I would have got more concern or sympathetic advice from any passerby in the street. Ginevra said nothing at all for some time. Then she asked why I had come to Munich.

"For an abortion, you must go to Sweden," she said. "Munich is very Catholic."

"I don't want an abortion."

"*Mein Gott*, Alex! That leaves adoption. If you're

putting a child up for adoption, there are Americans here who are looking to adopt.''

"That's what I hoped. Maybe you can help me find out how to go about it.''

"Yes . . .'' She sounded vague, as if she would prefer to have nothing to do with it. "I'll ask Rick to look into it discreetly, down at the Consulate. Who is the father?''

"That's classified information.''

Ginevra made a clicking noise with her tongue, reminding me of our mother. Clicking had been her way of expressing disgust and disbelief.

"Well, I'm sure you'll have to tell,'' she said. "Adoptive parents need to have some idea about heredity.''

"Then I'll just have to keep the baby.''

"Certainly not!'' Ginevra said, bursting with impatience. "You'll ruin your life and the kid's, too. Really, Alex, how in the world can you have been so stupid?''

Then she glanced at me again and must have seen how miserable I looked, because she said more gently, "Well, let's not worry. Rick will think of something. He always does.''

I was well aware that Ginevra and her husband, Richard Watkins, were dedicated toward a lofty goal. This post was Rick's big chance. He had reached the rank of FS-4, having started only a few years previously as a 7. From now on, everything he and his family did would be closely observed, duly noted on his Efficiency Report, and considered each time he came up for promotion. Between FS-4 and FS-1, the rank of ambassador, many were passed over or selected out. Ginevra had grown up seeing her mother's constant striving, and her father never quite measuring up to her expectations or to the State Department's. Rick was going to be different. Together they were going to be an ideal State Department couple. And there was no room in their careful plans for an errant younger sister.

Next day, capable Rick had all but arranged my life. There were many couples among the thousands of military and government Americans in Germany who wanted to adopt and who would not ask a lot of questions. Give him a week or two and he'd set it up.

"Rick is so wonderful," Ginevra said, relaxing at last. "We can stop worrying and have some fun together. You certainly don't look pregnant."

"That's because I've got about seven months to go." And as soon as I said that I suddenly realized what a long and unhappy time it was going to be. Part of me agreed with my sister that abortion was the best of the terrible choices. But I was still too close to David and my love for him, and I wanted that baby to have a life. I was like a person who, willingly and eagerly, has jumped into rough sea and has then remembered that she can't swim. Crazy. Inexplicable.

Ginevra kept trying to be kind and nice, but her true feelings showed.

"Oh, dear, Alex!" she said more than once. "You haven't *managed* well!" And managing was what Foreign Service women usually did so splendidly.

The third time she said it, we were in the breakfast room of her large, comfortable house in a Munich suburb, and she was spoon-feeding her youngest child. All her children were good-looking, healthy, and rather cowed. The baby's small receptive mouth opened wide for a spoonful of applesauce, then closed while Ginevra deftly scraped the spoon all around it, to remove all messy traces; then back to the dish; dip, feed, scrape. The baby became part of this machinelike procedure—receiving, swallowing. An automatic baby.

Everything else in Ginevra's household was as skillfully processed. An all-purpose servant set the table and after each meal washed the dishes. Ginevra cooked. In the evening, the servant converted into a nursemaid and put the children to bed. Then Ginevra turned from hausfrau to wife and comrade, asking Rick intelligent questions about the Bavarian elections, and showing familiarity with parties and candidates.

"We are invited to cocktails with the Engelhardts

tomorrow," she said to me, "and we'd love to have you come with us. The only thing is, the conversation will be in German and most likely the subject will be autobahn maintenance, because the Engelhardts are in the paving business. Will that interest you?"

"Well, not very much, thank you, Ginevra."

"Then perhaps you'd stay with the children. I owe Renate an evening off."

Once Ginevra and Rick had recovered from the shock and nuisance I had caused them, they seemed to enjoy helping me make decisions. The baby would be born in April, and I would need to find a pleasant, impersonal place to stay until then. Ginevra thought Salzburg might be a good idea—not too far from Munich and its good doctors. But I exasperated her by selecting Venice. I had childhood memories of a visit there. A pigeon had stood on my head in Piazza San Marco. I had loved the shop windows, twinkling with jewelry—amber, garnet, crystal. And the soothing sound of lapping water was everywhere you went.

"Venice will be damp, cold, rainy, and smelly," Ginevra objected. "And it's overnight from Munich. You'll wind up having the baby on the train."

"I'll come back here a month early," I said. "And I'll stay at some little pension near the hospital. You don't have to know I'm here."

"Suit yourself, then," she said. And added, "Just as you usually do."

Suit yourself as you usually do. I thought, I would be likely to say the same thing to David. We are not unlike. We suit ourselves, even when what we do is destructive. The difference is, I harm myself, but David goes free.

By the following week, Rick had selected parents for my baby, and it had been arranged for them to stand by in April to pick it up as soon as it had been born. Now I had one more job to do. Oz knew I was visiting my sister; now I had to write to him, breaking our engagement. I told him that I had felt for some time that it wouldn't work; that since my mother's death I had been depressed and needed to spend time in Europe, traveling and maybe studying, but living on my own. I asked him not to look for me, and I said that he should get on with his own life and forget me, because I was really not the right person for him. A couple of weeks later, an answer came. It was short and reserved, simply asking me to get in touch with him anytime I changed my mind.

In the years since that time, I have strictly avoided thinking about the winter I spent in Venice and the birth of the baby. Now, even if I try, I cannot remember it very well. Loneliness was the worst of it. I had stuck to my decision not to tell David—or at least not until much later—and it was not a tale for casual friends. Had my mother been alive, I would have gone to great lengths to prevent her from knowing; and Ginevra was no use at all. I had never liked secrets, because they seemed like burdens. And now I had a lifelong burden.

Venice suited my mood, because its story seemed to match my own. Once filled with energy and passion, now it seemed to look sadly back at the past and uncertainly at the future. I found a small *pensione* and settled down with a satchelful of paperbacks from an English-language bookshop in Munich. My room overlooked a back canal, so that I could hear, day and night, the lapping-water sounds that I remembered, and they still had the effect of making me feel soothed and tranquil.

While the weather continued fine, I wandered through the mazey streets, visited all the museums and dozens of churches, and took canal rides on the vaporetto. Several times I spent the day at the Lido, walking on the wide brown beach and wading in the Adriatic, still warm from summer. In November, I walked the rainy Venetian streets, in my maternity raincoat, under a streaming umbrella. I didn't care how cold the rain was, but I grew apprehensive when the Piazza San Marco began to flood, and people had to walk across it on makeshift bridges made of hastily laid-down planks. The cafes closed because their doors could not be opened without admitting a flood. That, too, suited my state of mind. Disaster by rain; rain in a beautiful place. In this weather, the vaporetto was crowded and plunged up and down on the restless Grand Canal. When the backwash rose and fell against the peach-colored palaces, one saw their ungainly foundations: precarious piles of brick, festooned with weeds.

It seemed that I must be the one lonely person in Venice. All the other foreigners, mostly Japanese or German, moved about in packs. Agile Japanese gentlemen risked soaking their neat trouser cuffs as they leaped over puddles to take pictures. German honeymoon couples crowded the bead shops, taking hours to select a glass necklace or two. On a rainy day I bought a necklace of blue glass, priced lower than when I had noticed it before on a sunny day, sparkling in the window. The beads were the blue of a Tiepolo sky, with flecks and bubbles here and there, suggesting wispy clouds. I took it "home"—that is, to my *pensione* room, and hung it on the lampshade, so that it would sparkle when the light was on. With methods like these, I got through the winter.

The *pensione* had other guests who, like me, were staying for weeks or months. As the days grew shorter and our rooms chillier, we tended to gather in the little *salone* before dinner, pulling our chairs close to a minute coal fire. Gradually, the others revealed themselves, or rather, small glimpses of themselves. One elderly lady from Ohio was thinking of becoming a glassblower. She went every day to a factory where she had persuaded them to give her lessons. A mother and daughter from Sweden had come to Italy to escape the stern Baltic winter, and in chilly December they were still going over to the Lido, where they actually put on their bathing suits and swam, while Italians watched dumbfounded. A plain-faced woman of about forty ("old maid" immediately came to my mind) was "just traveling"; and a married couple were on a sabbatical from a Michigan college.

As my pregnancy became obvious, I aroused the curiosity of all of them. My story was intricate: my husband was an officer in the Sixth Fleet, based in Naples. At present he was on Special Duty, the nature of which was a secret, even from me. And I had decided to come to Venice while I was waiting for him and for our baby. Why Venice? Well, I intended, some day, to get a degree in Art History, and my favorite painters were Titian and his contemporaries.

"Aren't you lonesome, all by yourself?" the glassblower asked me.

"No, I like being alone," I said. "I *prefer* it." That was to discourage them from trying to be nice to me.

One day, the Signora who owned the *pensione* came to me with glad news: there was another Navy wife arriving, a nice friend for me. Perhaps our husbands already knew each other. I immediately developed flu and did not leave my room until the Navy wife had left. I didn't think I could handle any more lies.

After several months had passed, I began to realize that something strange was happening to my emotions. I no longer had crying fits or felt terribly sorry for myself. In fact, I did not feel much of anything. And I thought of David only a few times a day instead of all the time. Physically I felt fine. Dr. Simoni, my obstetrician, said I was indeed fine, but warned against desserts. To that I paid no attention, and when the sun was out I used to sit at the Cafe Florio at an outdoor table, drinking a cappuccino and lingering over a whipped cream *dolce* of some kind.

One day in December, I bought a Christmas card with a picture of the Nativity and a *"Buon Natale"* message. Then I sat at my table debating what to say, finally writing "and Happy New Year, Alex." It was for Oz. I thought about adding "I'll be back in the spring," but I decided against getting anyone's hopes up—his or mine—and in the end I didn't send the card at all. Some part of me would have liked to feel something for Oz. Here was a man who had loved me and asked me to marry him, and I was grateful to him for that. He was not the Prince I had hoped for, but he had put himself in that role. It occurred to me that life is a lot like play-acting. You don't write the lines or direct the action, and you have to play your part with the actors that are there. It never occurred to me—then—that there might be another play I could be in.

With the detachment of a spectator rather than a player, I told myself that this was the worst year of my life, and things could only get better. I was surprised by my calm. The passion I had felt so totally seemed more like a storm that one reads about in the newspaper. A hundred thousand people swept away in Bangladesh: we have to turn aside because we can't undertake to feel agony a hundred thousand times. In a similar manner, I had turned aside from my own storm and its devastations.

When my baby grew bigger and stirred about vigorously, as if he (I always imagined "he") were not only alive but developing a personality, I thought about keeping him, but in those days this would have been a fairly rash step. I tried to imagine myself as an unwed mother ("single parent" had not yet entered the national vocabulary). Maybe, I thought, I could become the private secretary of a big executive, and make enough money to support my child and myself. But "what would people say" was a terror I couldn't get beyond. Furthermore, although I was ashamed to admit it to myself because it seemed unfemale, I was afraid

I wouldn't be much of a success as a mother. I observed Venetian mothers, responding totally and unstintingly to every whim of the little creatures in their arms, and I didn't think I could do it. Not all alone.

Being alone wasn't all bad, and my fellow boarders weren't bad either, but I did find myself longing for a real friend. And I found one in a history professor on sabbatical. Culver Turner was his name, and I somehow picked him up in the Doges' Palace. We made an unlikely couple—I pregnant, and he gay, both unmistakably so. But he liked a listener, and I loved to hear him talk from his vast knowledge of Venice in the Decadent Period. Together we went to obscure palaces and while we wandered through their icy rooms he would regale me, as if reminiscing, with bits of eighteenth-century gossip; about Count so-and-so and the half-dozen dwarves who were his constant companions; or about the all-night revels the Count used to give for masked guests. Culver made me see history. He could eliminate the postcard stands and the silken ropes protecting the chair seats, and bring in lighted candelabra, violins, murmuring voices, the clink of glasses, and the slap of cards. I responded to Culver's invocations and he was delighted. But in January his sabbatical was over and he had to return to his university.

"You'll have to rejoin the twentieth century," I remarked.

"Yes, but *you* don't have to. Go to the library and read about something. Something in the Renaissance. The eighteenth century is rather downbeat and you need cheering up. I recommend Caterina Cornaro."

"Who was she?"

"Find out," he said. "You'll like her."

After Culver left, I walked over to the library where he had been doing research and asked if I could work there. It was housed in an elegant old palazzo, unusually well heated, and I thought I would enjoy both the elegance and the heat.

A pleasant man at a reception desk read aloud from a pamphlet: "Our readers must have three letters of recommendation from recognized authorities. These are submitted to a committee. The applicant must also prove that the information he seeks can be found in no other library. Applications will receive a reply within six months."

I explained that I was staying in Venice temporarily and had no time to fulfill any of these requirements. He looked at my swollen front and asked when I would like to start.

"How about today?" I asked.

"*Va benissimo, Signora*," he said. "I will give you now a temporary card, good for three months. Please be at home."

I was amazed to discover how much I liked being there. Day after day, until the ninth month, I sat reading and note-taking at an enormous carved table. Gilt cherubs scampered across the ceiling, and were my only company except for an occasional pale scholar hunched over books in a far corner of the room. For the most part, the only sound I heard was of myself turning pages. Sometimes a heavy rain would pelt down into the flagged courtyard outside the window where I sat, and its intensity and the sudden darkening of the light seemed to suit my situation and my mood. To be away from people, dwelling inside my head, and surrounded by the trappings of other centuries and other mentalities seemed precisely what I needed. Another language, too, pleased me. I remembered some Italian from my childhood, and I also found someone to give me lessons twice a week.

I asked the librarian to bring me material on Caterina Cornaro, a fifteenth-century Venetian girl. The daughter of an important merchant prince, she was married at eighteen to the King of Cyprus. Four Venetian galleys conveyed Caterina and her dowry of gold and jewels to her new kingdom, but the marriage was ill-starred. The following year, she gave birth to a weakly son, who promptly died, and then the king died as well, and very soon another aspirant to the throne of this rich little island murdered most of the young queen's relations and supporters, and kept her a prisoner in her castle. After fifteen sad and lonely years, during which she paced the high parapets and surveyed but never visited her rocky kingdom, she was brought back to Venice by the Doge, who then established her as ruler of the tiny hill-town of Asolo. Here, she lived on for years as "La Regina Caterina," presiding over a miniature court that attracted poets, musicians, philosophers, and other persons versed in the culture of the times. But Venice was declining, losing territory, and in the end Queen Caterina was obliged to withdraw into the city itself, where she died in 1510.

While I sat in the library, reading about Caterina, my own unhappiness dwindled. It was hers I cared about. I learned that she grew fat, but was still considered beautiful; that she enjoyed elaborate clothes; and was generous to the poor but not to bad poets and mediocre painters. So wealthy and exalted a lady must have been courted, yet she remained a widow. If she had love affairs, they were conducted so discreetly as to leave no record. How sensible (I thought) to substitute learning for love.

Through the winter, I voyaged now and then to the Lido, warmly dressed, and walked on the deserted beach. I sensed that some of the passengers on the little ferry that took me there wondered about me, and that there was an element of concern in their wondering. They were not simply curious or nosy. They were solicitous. I felt that if I told my true story to one of them, I would hear sympathetic sighs and commiserations. Italians, in their ancient society, have seen everything, and can accept most of it with a shrug or an understanding smile. I knew that I had come to the right place, and therefore I wrote Ginevra that I would be having the baby there and to so advise the prospective parents.

Only Dr. Simoni evinced a touch of disapproval. Why, he wanted to know, did I not go to the Navy hospital in Naples, where I could be among my fellow Americans? Because, I said, I had heard how good Dottore Simoni was, here in Venice. I doubt if he believed that, or any of my story, but he took good care of me, and in April, a baby son was born, without long labor, in the hospital. My brother-in-law in the Munich Consulate-General shepherded the adoptive parents through a great deal of red tape. Sergeant and Mrs. Frank Costanza arrived in Venice without delay, and I only saw the baby once. I did not see the new parents at all, but I signed the papers they brought with them and then they whisked their son away. That was when I lost the sympathy of my doctor and the nurses. No matter what my story, how could I give up this beautiful *bambino*?

Back at the *pensione* I packed my bags, and told

the Signora that relatives had arrived to help me
and the baby travel to join my husband. The
Signora, who had counted on cooing over my baby
and dressing him in the little blue and pink sacque
she had been knitting, suddenly went very grim
and said good-bye without an embrace.

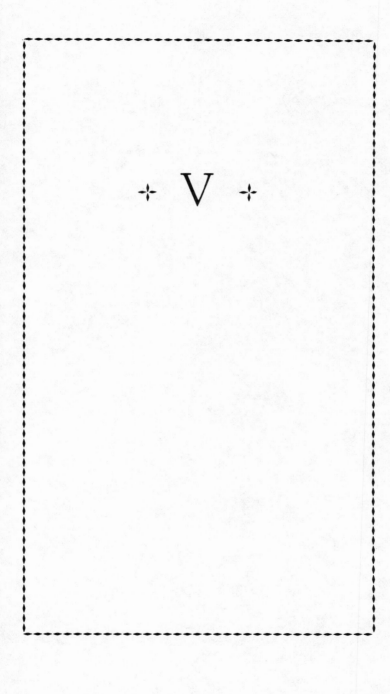

+ V +

I went back to New York, which had come to mean home to me, up to a point, and I went to work for another magazine. Then I found a roommate, who wanted to share her big, sunny apartment on the West Side, and gradually I felt able to close the door on the events of the year before. Well, almost. I looked in the telephone book to see whether David was listed, and he was. But I didn't dial the number. At Christmastime, on impulse, I sent a card to Oz, and he immediately answered with a letter saying that he was coming to New York.

And so we got back together. I was glad to see him and to hear him say, in his matter-of-fact and unloverly way, that he would still like to marry me. We were having dinner in a restaurant when he broached this subject.

"We need to have a long talk," I said, "in private."

"About what?"

"You don't know enough about me. Before you ask somebody to marry you, you ought to know all about her."

"Why? I know you all I need to."

I thought: how easy it would be not to tell him anything. Maybe I could tell him only that I've had a baby and given it away. I don't believe he could stand knowing the father is David. But if I don't tell him how can I live with it?

When he took me home, my roommate was out, so I tried again.

"I absolutely have to tell you something."

"I don't want to hear it," he said, and I could see that he was beginning to feel annoyed. "I don't want to hear any secrets and I don't want to tell mine."

I hadn't thought about *his* secrets. If he had secrets, maybe I could have mine without feeling guilty.

"Don't tell me anything you don't want to tell me," I said. "It's just that I'm nervous about skeletons falling out of the closet sometime in the future."

He was silent and I took that to mean that he would listen. I took a deep breath and said, "Oz . . ."

"No!" he interrupted, almost shouting. "We should begin right here. Begin by setting a wed-

ding date. If you've done something you regret, I
certainly have, too. I can't see any point in the
world in hashing things over. They're *finished.*"

I never did tell him. He never told me. Sometimes I wondered what his secrets were, but I was
unable to imagine anything important. He was
good old Oz, reliable and sweet-natured. He was
also only tepidly interested in sex. Anything so
disheveled, so out of control, troubled him. For
making love, he liked the light to be out and he
liked to wear pajamas. And he has always preferred twin beds, so that after the rather brief
event, he could leave me and get a good night's
rest.

Eighteen years later, we were still in the same
house where we first set up housekeeping. At first
I resisted the notion of living so near my in-laws,
but Oz quite reasonably pointed out that the house
was a good one and the rent was low. I took the
liberty of planting a lot of lilac bushes, for privacy,
between our house and the kitchen side of the
main house. I explained to Lydia that I didn't like
looking from our living-room window to a view of
her garbage cans, and she said she could understand that, but that I had chosen the wrong shrubs.
Evergreens would have been more practical, she
said.

"But I love lilacs," I said. "I wanted a forest of
them, and that's what I've got."

"Lilacs are perfectly splendid in Santa Fe when they have a good year," Lydia said. "But too often they get snowed on when they're budding, and then they look terrible."

"I'll take my chances," I said. When the spring is kind to them, these lilacs are the most beautiful of all my flowers. The bushes have grown tall and thick and, even in winter, form a good screen, and make me feel protected. Without them, we'd be seeing Mrs. Martinez and Filomena, stolidly sitting on the kitchen *portal* waiting for their employers to be ready to eat dinner. The dinner hour has grown later and later over at the main house, as Lydia and Deck have moved from social drinking to heavy drinking to alcoholism. Mrs. Martinez and her daughter have a lot of waiting around to do.

During the first year of my marriage, Lydia tried to involve me in her social and charitable interests. In those days she had many: besides ladies' lunches and bridge parties, she was a member of many boards and committees, where she was not only very good at getting things done, but reveled in the opportunity to tell people what to do. For a while she drew me into three of her favorite projects, Friends of the Sea Otter, Save the Whale, and Adopt a Burro. When Lydia took up a cause, she moved like a natural phenomenon of great force: an earthquake, a sandstorm, a tidal wave. It may have had something to do with being

rich and politically very conservative. Ever since
Franklin D. Roosevelt, she had felt her way of life
threatened and could therefore identify with a sea
otter strangling in a fisherman's net, or with a
whale struck down in its happy ocean by mechani-
cal harpoons. She *became* the otter and the whale.

About three years after Oz and I were married,
David and Bishy bought their cattle ranch in central New Mexico, about a two-hour drive from
Santa Fe. The first time they came to visit the
parents, Oz told me it would be nice if we invited
everyone to dinner. I had realized that this would
happen, sooner or later, so I didn't try to resist it.
I saw to it that our house looked very attractive
and that the dinner was delicious, and I tried to
look like a devoted, happy wife.

The last time I had seen David, we had said a
deeply sad good-bye at the Eighty-ninth Street
apartment. (Oz and I had not asked any family to
our wedding, which was hardly a wedding at all,
just a trip to City Hall, with two friends as
witnesses.) When David and Bishy arrived at our
house that evening, he gave me a big, long hug and
kissed me on both cheeks, and I was shocked at
how good it felt to be close to him. So I made an
excuse to hurry off into the kitchen, where I gave
myself a stern talking-to. Pretend this is a diplomatic dinner, I told myself. If all goes well, Oz
will get a promotion, and it all depends on his

wife. Don't burn anything, don't forget any-thing. Don't give an opinion or say anything in the least meaningful. And, above all, don't even *look* at David.

That worked pretty well, but the conversation at table went slowly. David was taciturn, and Bishy, who was pregnant after two miscarriages, had none of her old schoolgirlish chatter. I thought perhaps the transition from the East to the high plains of New Mexico had been too drastic a change.

"Bishy, my dear, you need to get into environmental concerns," Lydia told her.

"Well, I'm going to," Bishy said, "just as soon as I get used to things here. Things like centipedes crawling around the house."

"Centipedes are necessary to ecology, darling, but I can understand your not liking them. When you are settled, I'd like you on my Bring Back the Wolf committee."

"Wolves kill livestock, Mother," David said. "And I have a cattle ranch."

"They don't attack healthy stock," Lydia flashed back. "They only cull out the old and sick, and that's useful. I'll send you the literature."

"I don't want any literature," David said. "If I see a wolf I'll shoot it."

David was still his mother's darling and she didn't want to argue with him.

"Davey, you know how I am about protecting

animals," she said. "I can't help it, I have always been a kind person. I was the only girl in my class at Farmington who burst into tears and had to leave the room when they showed us a movie of Roosevelt and his trophies. I always hated that man."

"Franklin?" Oz asked.

"Of course not. *Nobody* liked Franklin, but I'm talking about Theodore. He *hunted*. He even brought his disgusting bison heads into the White House, so I've heard. Dripping with blood, no doubt."

"So you were a nonconformist at school," I said. "I never thought of you as that."

Deck said admiringly, "She always has been. She makes things spin, that one."

Lydia looked pleased by this endorsement.

"I make things *happen*," she said.

"We know you do, Ma," Oz said cheerfully.

But the mention of hunting had reminded her that Oz was a hunter.

"One thing I'd like to make happen *now*," she said, glaring at Oz, "is, to get you to stop hunting. I feel disgraced, especially since I'm trying so hard to save animals from cruelty and death, that my own son is out there in the woods with a big rifle."

Oz always looked depressed when his mother scolded him. I knew that nothing she said would ever make him give up hunting, which was one of his few enthusiasms, but after she frowned at him he said nothing more for the rest of the meal.

Before David and Bishy went back to their ranch, I found an opportunity to get David alone for a minute, and I handed him a sealed manila envelope, containing the adoption papers.

I said, "I thought a long time about whether to give you these. It will be a shock. But I guess I just need to do this and I'm hoping that it's best for you."

"What is it?" he asked.

"You'll see. And wait till you're alone to open it. Nobody in this family knows about what's in that envelope, and nobody in the world knows, except the people directly involved. It's a dead secret, and I'm trusting you to keep it that way."

I didn't wait to see him open the envelope. The papers gave the baby's new name and that of his new parents, but I had taken a pair of scissors and carefully cut out my name. David's did not appear at all.

A few days later, he called me. It was during the day, when he knew Oz would be at work. I told him right away that there was no point in our discussing anything.

"Then why did you decide to tell me at this particular time?"

"I was always going to tell you sooner or later,

and this just seemed like a—well, a convenient opportunity."

"Convenient! Alex, my God—why wasn't it convenient when you found out you were pregnant? When you were going through something terrible and I should have been there?"

I felt a lump in my throat, so I was silent until I had pulled myself together. Meantime he said, "Did you suppose I wouldn't care?"

I took a deep breath and said, "You couldn't have done anything about it."

Now it was he who was silent. "I could have been there for you," he finally said in a low voice.

"Not even that, I'm afraid. Look, David, it's over. Don't worry. I'm fine now and so are you and so, I'm sure, is the baby."

"I want to see you."

"Oh, no!" I said instantly, beginning to be apprehensive. "David, if you really feel like doing something to help me, just do nothing. Don't try to see me, don't talk to me, don't tell anyone. Especially not Bishy."

"Of course not. But—"

"Just put it all aside. Forever. Everybody's fine now. Good-bye. I'm going to hang up." And I did.

Then I sat there by the telephone, looking out the window at the aloof mountain peaks, and cried hard. I knew I had done the right thing and I felt pleased with myself for having behaved in an adult manner. But the tears were for matters much more profound than proper behavior: lost love, lost passion, and the tenderness I had heard in David's voice.

When I first went to Santa Fe to live, the only thing that felt normal about it was the fact that I had moved, once again, into a new and puzzling atmosphere. Moving had always seemed like a giant eraser, rubbing out the life before. In this case the eraser rubbed out New York, rubbed out David, rubbed out Venice. A similar eraser had served my mother, who had prided herself on leaving every house where we had lived exactly as she had found it, just as though the Burrows family had never been there at all.

Foreign Service people had one advantage when they moved. Wherever they went, they already had membership in an exclusive club—the Foreign Service—and they were united by their flag—the Stars and Stripes. When I was a child, the sight of that bright flag gave me a comforting feeling when I saw it flying over one of our embassies or consulates, or at the stern of a motorboat in Bangkok, or on the fender of our ambassador's official car. Poor foreigners, I would think. They are not American. Then I grew up and discovered that millions of people did not share my views and that some of

them actually wanted to set fire to that flag or burn
down those embassies. It took me a long time to
perceive that the United States had drawbacks.
When I finally grasped that basic fact, I was able to
say good-bye to certain arrogant illusions, but I
still liked being American.

As a little girl, I used to hear my mother's
friends complaining about life in hardship posts—
Saudi Arabia, say, or Cambodia, and other places
where the State Department sought to mitigate the
hardships of its representatives with twenty per
cent more pay. Now, in my post at Santa Fe, I
wondered whether it was more of a hardship trying
to communicate with people whose native tongue
was Arabic or Khmer than with a husband like
Oz, who understood English perfectly but did not
enjoy communicating.

One reason that Oz and I got along as well as
we did was that we both disliked a fuss. We kept
our darker sides firmly locked away. I figured out
that his fondness for hunting was due to the free-
dom it gave him to be aggressive. In all areas of his
life—with his mother, with me, and with people
in the bank—he was a nice guy. But in the woods,
I was sure, the bullets he fired at the deer also
served to annihilate difficult bank customers, school-
teachers he hadn't liked, and (could it be?) close
members of his family.

I don't know how much Oz minded that we

never had children. For a while we tried all the recommended medical procedures for conception, but nothing happened. I would have liked to adopt, but Oz said no, perhaps influenced by Lydia, who was dead against it. "Blood will tell" was one of her mottoes. And no waif or stray, up for adoption, could possibly measure up to the aristocratic Smithsons, especially since Smithson blood had been enhanced by that of Lydia Aspinwall.

I tried to please Oz and to be easy to live with. I cooked a lot, sewed on buttons, even shined Oz's shoes. I knitted sweaters and needle-pointed waistcoats. And in the rest of my time I gardened and took courses. Perhaps I became addicted to learning while in that Venetian library; it seemed to do for me what alcohol does for some people. Through the years I've studied Spanish, Birds of the Southwest, Eighteenth-century Antiques, Chinese Cooking, Haiku, Belly-dancing, Creative Writing, How to Understand Your Car, Italian, and Beginning Watercolor. As a matter of fact, all my courses except Italian have been for beginners; I seldom seem to become Advanced. In addition, I have attended probably a dozen seminars. Homer, Shakespeare, Dante, Jane Austen, Nineteenth-century Lyric Poets, all now faded in my memory like yesterday's sunsets, except for vivid bits from here or there that have lasted with me. Dante, for instance: ". . . The love that moves the sun and the other stars."

Oz and I had one big thing in common: we were both brought up with too many parties going on around us. During the first dozen years or so of our marriage the parties at Gallegos Ranch continued. Lydia and Deck were relentless entertainers, and although we gradually stopped going to their parties, or being invited, in summertime we could plainly hear the laughter. Old-timers used to tell me about the good old days in the 1930s and 1940s, when the annual Fiesta, in early September, had not yet turned commercial. The Anglo community was then small enough so that everyone in it knew everyone else, and just about all of them gave Fiesta parties. The Smithson parties began at noon and went on far into the evening, with barbecued sides of beef, and mariachi bands, and impromptu polo games, played on quarter horses by Deck and visiting buddies from the East.

As Lydia and Deck grew older, they still gave exuberant, inebriated gatherings, even though they and their friends were getting to the point where the gatherings turned out more inebriated than exuberant. Next day the lawn would be strewn with cigarette butts, paper napkins, and perhaps a martini glass or two, or a lost earring. Once, in the lilac bushes, I came upon the president of Oz's bank, who had dozed off there the night before.

After Deck lost his driver's license, he had to stay home more, but he didn't seem to mind. He could pass out in his own library chair and not have to be carried anywhere. Then Lydia stopped driving, drunk or sober, because of cataracts, and when they went out their elderly Mercedes was driven by Filomena. Sometimes old friends came to share that treasured time of day, the cocktail hour, but Lydia and Deck were happy enough by themselves. The important thing for them, the only important thing at that time of day, was the ice bucket and the innocent-looking, water-colored liquid that flowed from bottles labeled gin.

For all their token enthusiasm about the Southwest, the elder Smithsons were still from Rhode Island. Oz told me once that when his parents stopped changing for dinner he had supposed they had psychologically moved West. But no. They still went back to Providence every year to stay with cousins and they still called it "going home." In summer at Gallegos Ranch they would sit on their *portal* at sunset-time, watching the Sangre de Cristo Mountains turning blood-red in reflected light, and the clouds of the enormous western sky seething with colors seldom seen in New England —at least, not all at once—deep pinks, violent reds, savage yellows, fierce oranges.

Lydia might say, "Think, Deck, if we didn't live in New Mexico, we wouldn't be seeing these sunsets." And yet it was always clear that these skies were not their skies. Here, they were "from away."

Once, in a sudden fever of enterprise, I asked

Oz if he didn't want me to give a dinner party for his colleagues and superiors at the bank.

"What for?" he inquired.

"So you'll be on good terms with them—and get ahead—and—" At that point I faltered, because he was looking at me in such surprise.

"I *am* on good terms with them," he said. "I *am* ahead."

I said no more. Oz had made it clear that he wasn't interested in the social side of life, and he had no need of social climbing because in Santa Fe the Smithsons were already at the top. Anyway, Santa Fe has no ranking system, in either the eastern-seaboard sense or the Foreign Service sense, but only many small cliques, some of which interlock with others. Citizens of Spanish descent have their own social hierarchies; and a certain special respect is accorded to Anglo families who, like the Smithsons, are "old-timers," meaning those who have been here for more than a generation. Still, anyone with a reasonably pleasant personality and plenty of money, who will spend some of it on lavish entertaining and contribute substantial sums to the Santa Fe Opera, can be at the top of any clique he or she chooses.

I asked myself why I continued to give shelf space to my mother's party paraphernalia. The twenty-four lacquer finger bowls I had saved from her things now gathered dust on a top shelf, along with forty-three Waterford wineglasses and eleven gold-rimmed Spode plates. I felt stupid for being unable to part with them, and I decided it must be because they had given continuity to my disjointed childhood. I had seen them packed and unpacked on four continents, and each time they had emerged from their packing boxes I had experienced the same sense of comfort as when I greeted my dolls and my teddy bear after they, too, had made a long trip by sea or freight train. I depended on them for the reassurance that I, like they, had a unique existence and could survive anywhere. I had also felt closer to my mother when I saw her lift her treasures from their wrappings and put them away in whatever new house or apartment we were moving into. And when she tucked me into a new bed and turned off the lights in an unfamiliar bedroom, I had felt reassured that I, too, was a treasure worth saving.

As I grew older, I sometimes questioned this reverence for possessions. Once, when my mother and I were moving into the East Eighty-ninth Street apartment, I asked her, "Why are we saving these old napkins with holes in them?"

My mother answered—astonishingly—"There is nothing like old linen for bandages."

"Are you expecting a nuclear attack?" I inquired, in the nasty manner that often comes over teenagers.

But my mother stood her ground. "You never

know what will happen," she said, and found a place for a pile of ragged double-damask. At that point I realized, for the first time, that this mother who seemed so capable and full of common sense was also prey to shadowy terrors. And for the first time I felt compassionate—a little less absorbed in my own fears, a little more aware of someone else's.

Parties were certainly one source of my fears, even though I was thoroughly programmed to attend them. As a child, when my parents entertained and I was there to pass hors d'oeuvres, I felt doubly an outsider. One, because most of the people in the room were speaking other languages, and, two, because of being a child. The guests would accept from me a cracker spread with something fancy, and perhaps would say, "What a pretty dress you have!" or "What a good little hostess!" I learned superficiality from being at those parties, and I can still summon it up when it seems fitting. But I was play-acting then and I still am. And I still grow fearful at parties, remembering my travels around big rooms, gripping, at a slightly tipped angle, a tray of canapes, and forging my way through towering groves of people I had never seen before.

In those days, I longed to be a pretty, grown-up girl, smiling and chattering, and brandishing a cigarette. One time, in Africa, I saw two of our guests slip out through the French doors that led to a terrace. I followed them, and saw that one was the wife of our new vice-consul and the other a Greek consulate official whose child was in my class at school. They were kissing intensely. I had never seen such kissing. This was before the days of TV soap operas, and my parents rarely kissed in my presence, intensely or not. I reported this incident to them—I was then five—and my father told me about the monkeys who could "hear no evil, see no evil, speak no evil." He said that this should be the motto of a Foreign Service child, and to emphasize the point, he bought me a little charm, with those discreet animals carved in bone. Someone in our Consulate circle must have been less discreet than the monkeys, however, because not long afterward our vice-consul and his out-of-line wife were suddenly transferred.

Although I was so young, I knew that this woman would be getting a low rating when it came time for the annual Efficiency Reports. A wife who was rated gauche, inept, dull-witted, intemperate, grumpy, mannerless, or a "security risk"—that is, open to gossip or blackmail—could drag her husband down. Stories were told of even the most capable of Foreign Service Officers who had been passed over for high posts because the little woman wouldn't do. I also knew that my mother was rated "an Asset," and in Santa Fe I compared myself unfavorably with her until I finally realized that my "performance" had nothing to do with Oz and his bank.

Sometimes, in Santa Fe, I had to remind myself that I was there to stay, that I was not going anywhere. This seemed unnatural. When I made friends, I noticed that I held something back, as though I didn't expect to know them long. And when I planted lilacs, to shield myself from the in-laws, I couldn't imagine the day when the bushes would be ten feet high and I'd still be here to see them.

Five years or so into my marriage, I began to suffer from bouts of sadness, sometimes so acute that I would do nothing but lie on my bed most of the day. Oz's only suggestion was "snap out of it," but when I failed to snap out, I decided to see Dr. Fischer, a psychiatrist. The first session or two went well, but when he began asking awkward questions, I found myself apprehensive.

He was the kind of psychiatrist who doesn't put his patients on a couch, but seats them by his desk. Looking straight at his cheery, well-adjusted face, I felt like a child who has been sent to see the principal.

"Well now, Alexandra," he said, leaning back in his large, authoritarian's chair. "Are you ever angry because you and your husband live in his parents' guesthouse, literally a stone's throw from a mother-in-law you can't stand?"

"I guess so," I said. "But the rent is low, it's a nice house, Oz likes it, and I hate moving."

He said that those answers sounded evasive, and I responded rather tartly that if I were good at giving direct answers I wouldn't need a psychiatrist.

"*That* was a fine, direct answer," he said. "You really told me off. So it's clear that you can assert yourself if you want to."

"But I don't want to," I said. "Usually I'm very polite and eager to please. I was brought up that way."

"And do you like being that way?"

"Maybe not, but I don't know how to be different."

"What would you choose as an epitaph? 'Alexandra Smithson . . . She was polite and eager to please'?"

"Certainly not."

"Does that notion make you feel anxious? Angry?"

I looked at my watch. "I feel that it's time to go home," I said.

"We have fourteen more minutes," he said firmly. "Please relax. I'd like to hear some early memories about being a good girl and pleasing everyone. What comes to mind in regard to that?"

I closed my eyes, sighed, and saw late autumn on a Florentine hillside, with the roses gone from the garden and the paths soggy with wet yellow leaves. We were packing to move, after two happy years in Florence, to the next post, which was going to be Hamburg. My mother had tears in her eyes as she folded curtains and took down pictures and decided what to throw away. Florence had been the pleasantest post yet, and she clearly felt that Hamburg would be like being cast into outer darkness. Taking a cue from her, I feared it would be outer darkness for me, too, although as far as I knew, Hamburg was only a place where they ate a lot of hamburgers.

Then a friend told me that Hamburg was in Germany, where the Nazis lived. That night I had a nightmare about them. I screamed, and when my mother came to my bedside, I told her that we couldn't go to Germany, because the Nazis would mow us down with machine guns.

My mother took me on her lap and rocked me. "Don't be silly—the Nazis are gone now. Everything will be fine," she said. Somehow I knew she didn't quite mean that, and that my nightmare could as well have been hers.

She went on, "Don't you like stuffed animals? Wonderful cuckoo clooks? Germany is where they come from. And there's a famous zoo in Hamburg. You and I will have lots of fun together."

"But it's fun *here*. I wish we could stay."

"Hamburg will be a big step up for Daddy and we must help him all we can."

137

Yes, I knew about that: that fathers and husbands needed all kinds of help. If they didn't get it, they wouldn't like you anymore, and neither would the Efficiency Report people in Washington.

Hamburg in winter was the darkest place I had ever been to. The sun was not fully up until about nine in the morning, and it began to head for the horizon soon after three. Now I thought I knew what my mother must have meant when she spoke of outer darkness.

The day after we arrived, I went into the backyard of our new house, exploring. The ground was a sad expanse of frozen snow, most of it too hard to give way when I walked on it. Icicles hung from a clothesline. Drifts submerged a children's playhouse that looked like the witch's hut in *Hansel and Gretel*. And a round, dull-yellow sun, like a big wafer of butterscotch, sank rapidly through bare trees. I thought, we can't stand it here.

As always, Mother and Daddy were going out for cocktails, and a sitter had been hastily found for me. She was a grouchy teenager who spoke no English and who sat in the living room, playing the radio, while I put myself to bed upstairs. Later, I was awakened by my parents coming in, lively from the drinks they'd had (but not drunk, never that). Their voices sounded happy, as if this weren't Outer Darkness after all. They'd met such nice people, including delightful Germans. And now they had some invitations. Mother must quickly unpack her engagement book, I heard her say.

I knew then that she and I would not be spending much time at the zoo, or shopping for stuffed bears and cuckoo clocks. She was going to start helping Daddy, and so was I: performing my usual chores of passing hors d'oeuvres, smiling at everyone, and being a good girl. And that was what life was all about.

Oz was very much annoyed when I told him about Dr. Fischer. He said that we couldn't afford it, and that anyway, psychiatry was a racket. I canceled my visits, but, soon afterward, I drove down to the University in Albuquerque and signed up for an art history course. I had not even consulted Oz about it, and he wasn't very pleased when I told him.

"If you have to study something," he said, "why not economics or accounting? I could help you with things like that."

"Sorry," I said, "but this is what I'm going to do." And I wished Dr. Fischer were there to hear this. Nevertheless, guilt and unease soon overtook me, and I started knitting a new sweater for Oz that very evening.

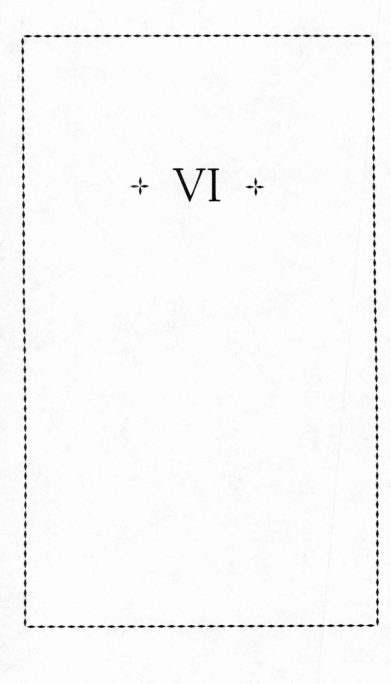

+ VI +

The telephone numbers of the main house and of our house were similar and sometimes people confused them. A few mornings after the newspaper article, I answered my phone and it was Bishy, calling Lydia from New York. When she realized she'd reached me instead, she said, "Oh, well, then, please give her a message. Tell her I'm coming back to New Mexico today and I'd like to stay with her tonight."

Bishy and I had never developed any empathy, but we were always scrupulously pleasant to each other.

I said, "Bishy, Lydia won't like missing your call. Why don't you dial again?"

"No," Bishy said. "She knows I'm coming today or tomorrow. Just tell her I'll be there late today. And not to bother about supper. I won't be hungry. Good-bye, Alex."

Next morning, Lydia called and said, "Alex my dear, please come right over."

Alex *my dear*. And *please*. Lydia must be up to something, I thought. And I was sure of it when she added, "This is of the greatest importance, Alexandra. As a matter of fact, it is *imperative*."

That kind of talk was not like her. I canceled a lunch date in town and crossed the lawn to the main house.

Bishy and I greeted each other tepidly, as usual.

"Hello, Alex," Bishy said. "How's Oz?"

"Fine," I said. "How's David?"

"I've been in the East," she said, "so I really don't know."

I wondered if she also meant "and I really don't care." It sounded that way.

Bishy had not lost her ingenue good looks, and she still wore her hair fastened with a child's barrette. Since the tragedy of her little son, she no longer seemed a sheltered young girl who deserved and expected nothing but the best. Her eyes, which used to say "Life is perfectly lovely" now said something like "What happened? Where is the perfectly lovely life?" Even when I remembered our disagreeable encounter on that long-ago New Year's morning, I could no longer seriously dislike her. I felt sorry for her.

"How about a glass of something?" Lydia asked. "A Bloody Mary?"

"No, thank you," I said.

"A little sherry? Campari and soda?"

"Thanks, but no."

"Deck has gone to town for his dentist appointment. He mixed a little batch of Bloodies before he went, so we may as well finish them off. Do sit down, girls."

We were in the library. As usual, there was no order there. The dog was in Deck's chair, and we had to move papers and miscellany from the sofa before it was possible to sit on it.

"Bishy has come bearing tidings," Lydia began. "In regard to David's awful legal action, she has found something we can do about it."

"Terrific," I said, and looked inquiringly at Bishy. There was definitely something too pleasant in Lydia's manner and in Bishy's, and intuition told me that whatever was in the wind was going to require my cooperation.

Lydia took a long swig from her glass and said, "Since it's quite a delicate matter, and I'm rather an old lady, I'll let Bishy tell it."

"It's not easy, Alex," Bishy said, taking the floor. "I realize that I'm being disloyal to David, but it can't be helped. He's doing something insane, going to court like this, and he's got to be stopped. And it occurred to me that the reason— the *real* reason—why our parents-in-law have decided to leave the property outside the family is because neither of their sons have heirs. They always pictured the ranch handed down in the family, generation after generation, like an English castle."

"Quite right," Lydia said. "Or like the houses in Providence that belonged to our ancestors. All of them are still in the hands of descendants. Even the house where Deck and I lived when we were first married we sold to a cousin."

"However," Bishy said, and I saw her hands grip the arms of her chair, "*However*! Only recently—about a year ago, I guess—I learned something that no one else knows except David." And she paused dramatically. "There *is* a male heir."

I looked back at her steadily, waiting.

"David had a son out of wedlock. That child was adopted and must now be about nineteen."

This came as such a shock to me that I could not help but show it. Finally I said, as calmly as possible, "How do you know?"

"Last year David was away and I simply had to find some papers in his file. So while I was looking through, I came upon the adoption papers. They showed that "Baby Boy," born in Venice, Italy, had been adopted by Sergeant Frank Costanza and wife, of New Haven, Connecticut. They'd named the child Vincent."

I said, "But that doesn't say anything about David."

"No, the names of the real parents had been cut out. But when David got home I showed him the papers, and he said yes, the baby was his."

Lydia chimed in, "And he won't say who the mother was. Italian, I suppose. Deck says it's very gentlemanly of David not to tell, but I must say I'd like to know. Maybe he'll tell us later."

"I doubt that," I said.

"Well, I think he will, because we're going to bring that boy to New Mexico and if Deck and I like him, we've decided to leave the property to our sons, in trust for this grandson."

I could think of nothing appropriate to say, and Lydia went on, "It's amazing to me to have a grandson with an Italian name because, of course, when I was growing up in Providence there was nothing lower than wops. But, of course, he's not really one, and he'll take the name of Smithson. I certainly don't care for that name Vincent. Doesn't sound like *us*, and I'll suggest a change. Anyway, Bishy's hired a detective and now we know where the boy is: right in New Haven, Connecticut."

"Thanks for telling me, and I'll let Oz know," I said, rising to leave. "I really don't need to hear anymore."

"I'm afraid—" Bishy said, "that you'll have to hear more. Because we want you to go and find him. Get him and bring him here."

"Nonsense," I said quickly. "That's for you and Lydia to do, since it's your idea."

"*I* can't go anywhere," Lydia said. "I'm too old and tired. So is Deck. As for Bishy—well, I really don't think we can ask her to look for her husband's bastard. I mean, that would be the ultimate cruelty. I know—and you must know, too, Alex, dear—that Oz would never do it. So it has to be you."

"Why not David?"

"Absolutely not. He says he'll have nothing to do with it."

"Neither will I. It's absurd."

"Do it for Oz," Bishy put in suddenly. "You know he loves this place. Do it to get rid of the Glorious Lighters."

I had to admit to myself that she had made a telling point. I liked to please Oz, because pleasing him alleviated the guilt I felt toward him. I also wanted to safeguard the property. I told Lydia and Bishy that I'd be willing to give the subject more thought and get back to them later. Then I walked back to our house.

I found myself surprised to find it still there, with a stew I'd left on the stove peacefully simmering; because I felt as if a tornado had come along and that nothing was ever going to be the same.

It was a sultry late-May afternoon in New Haven, the sun somewhere up there behind the smog. The new summer leaves were already dusty. I waited in a rented car on a street that had never been fashionable and wasn't now, near a classroom building at the University of New Haven.

Bishy's detective, Mr. Ryan, had told me exactly where to find Vincent Costanza, and he'd given me a snapshot of him, plus a written description:

> *Six feet tall, husky build, a little overweight*
> *Blue eyes*
> *Medium blond curly hair*
> *Smiles a lot, Good teeth*
> *Probably will be wearing jeans and a T-shirt, maybe with "University of New Haven" on it, or a duck, with "The duck stops here"*
> *Owns a navy blue knapsack*
> *May be wearing blue running shoes.*

In addition, Mr. Ryan had told me that Vincent usually left the college shortly after three o'clock and would be walking home along this street. He lived three blocks away.

A strange emotional state had come over me, much like the one I had lived through in Venice. It was a kind of spiritual numbness and shock, which allowed me to drive the car and get to the right place at the right time, but not to comprehend what was truly happening. I was about to meet a young stranger in whom elements of myself and of David had been living, intermingled, for two decades. The blue eyes (David's) and the blond hair (mine) would be obvious, but I knew that if there were qualities, mannerisms, interests, personality traits that I would recognize, I would be grateful for this numb feeling. I was determined that he would see me as a messenger and nothing more. At least, for the present.

I sat in the car, with the air-conditioning on, and very soon after three, the almost deserted sidewalk began to be busy with young people. On this side of the street, there were tennis courts and a parking lot. Opposite stood a long line of venerable three-deckers, built for working-class people at the turn of the century. To arrive here, I had passed through street after street of the same sort of houses. Some had carefully tended yards, with statues of gnomes or the Virgin Mary, beds of canna, and rose-of-Sharon bushes. Some had vegetable gardens. Some were taken up by children's wading pools of blue plastic, barbecue equipment, tetherball poles.

According to Mr. Ryan, the Costanzas had lived in this neighborhood ever since Frank Costanza had left the Army soon after the adoption, so this would be the only home Vincent would remember. Ryan had given me the street and number of his parents' house, but advised me to contact Vincent directly. In many cases such as this, he said, the adoptive parents would manage to sabotage any contact between child and biological parent.

"You never know," he had said. "Some of them are real defensive. They figure it's their kid, their property. Some of them don't even tell a child he's adopted, but, according to my sources, the Costanzas did. Vincent knows, and so do all their family and friends."

It was strange indeed for me to sit there, looking for my son whom nobody knew was my son. It seemed to me that I felt no intimations of mother love for the pleasant, slightly overweight (like my father) boy in the snapshot. And I hoped I wouldn't.

There were soon many young people walking by, and I stepped out of the car for fear of missing Vincent, but he was unmistakable. Curly hair, blue knapsack, dirty blue running shoes, a duck on his T-shirt.

"Vincent Costanza?" I asked, and he nodded, looking startled. "My name is Alexandra Smithson. I'm a—friend—of friends of yours and I need to talk to you for a few minutes."

He looked at me with, yes, David's blue eyes, but with a guileless stare in them. Unsophisticated, I thought—which would never have been a word I'd have used for David. I got the impression of a young man who had led an uneventful life.

"Sure," he said. "What's going on?"

I had pondered for some time about what to say at this point and I had it prepared.

"Why don't we go and have a milk shake? That way we'll be more comfortable."

151

He looked even more surprised, but again said, "Sure."

At the end of the block was a Burger King. When we were settled with milk shakes, I forged ahead with my mission. "I know this will be a shock to you," I said, "but I hope not a bad shock. I am representing your biological family and they have asked me to get in touch with you."

For half a minute he was speechless, staring at me wide-eyed. I began to fear that he had never been told he was adopted, but he finally said, "You mean the people who *had* me. Wow! Have you talked to my mom and dad?"

"Well, you are grown up," I pointed out— though he scarcely seemed so, "and free to make your own decisions. We thought it would be better to approach you privately to see what you might feel like doing."

"Like doing what? Are you saying I could meet my—you know, other mom?"

"Actually, it's your grandmother who is anxious to see you. And your grandfather."

"Not my other mom?" A slight strain came into his voice. "Is she dead?"

This was the hard part. "Vincent, I'm sorry, but we don't know where she is. Your father is alive, but—well, he may not be available. But your grandparents have been wanting for years to see you. They just waited until you were grown up."

But he seemed to be getting even *less* grown-up. Like a child, he kept banging his shoe against the table leg and winding a finger through his curly hair.

"Where are these people?" he asked. "I'm broke. I can't go very far."

"Don't worry about that. They'll buy your plane ticket. To New Mexico."

He began to seem more interested. "Cool," he said.

There was a silence, during which he noisily sucked up the last of his milk shake.

"Do people call you Vincent? Or a nickname?" I asked.

"Vincent—or Vince, sometimes."

"Your mother was born in Genoa, is that right?"

"How did you know?"

I wanted to tell him as few lies and as much of the truth as possible. "Your birth family hired a detective to find you. We already knew that you had been adopted by Frank Costanza and his wife, Teresa, in New Haven."

"Yeah. Dad was stationed in Italy right after the War and he and Mom met at a dance. Dad was born right here in New Haven." He smiled, a smile that was something like David's, except that his face was so much rounder. "And what about my—you know, father? What's he like?"

A hard question. "He looks something like you,"

I said. "But, Vincent, I have to remind you that it's your grandparents—his father and mother—who want to see you. You see, there is a problem about an inheritance."

"What kind of problem?" he asked quickly, now beginning to look very interested.

I thought, maybe he's not so childish after all.

"Your grandparents will tell you about it," I said. "It's not up to me. I'm only—only a sort of messenger."

"Are you related to me?"

"I'm married to your father's brother."

"Were my father and mother married?"

"No."

He scowled. "My mom and dad told me they were, only they were too poor to keep me."

"Adoptive parents often say things like that, so the child won't be wondering where his biological parents are."

"They said I was born in Italy. So, was my mother Italian?"

That was painful for me to deal with. "It's a possibility, isn't it?" I finally said.

Suddenly, all this seemed a lot for him to take. He swallowed, bent his head, seemed almost on the verge of tears.

I said, "I know it's a lot to lay on you all at once."

He shook his head slowly. "At least my—those

two people—didn't get an abortion. I don't believe in that. Imagine, if that lady had, *I wouldn't be here!*"

"Right! Terrible thought!" And we both managed a laugh. "So, what do you want to do, Vincent? Will you come and see your birth grandparents?"

It came over me that this whole thing was very hard on me and I began to hope he might say no. But I had done my job all too well.

"Well, yeah, I guess," he said. "But right now, I'm about to have exams."

"Yes, but we have Memorial Day weekend coming up. We could leave tomorrow and have you back Tuesday."

"Okay. Except"—he looked anxious—"I'll have to ask Mom and Dad."

"Ask them, of course, tell them everything, but don't forget—you're of age. You make your own decisions now, don't you?"

"Yeah, sometimes. They may not mind, anyway. They know I love them."

I gave him the telephone number of the motel where I was staying. "Call me this evening," I said, "and we'll arrange all the details for the trip."

As we left Burger King, he asked, "Where did you say these folks live?"

"In New Mexico."

"Are they Mexicans?"

155

"*New* Mexico, Vince." He looked blank and I added, "It's one of the fifty states."

"Oh, that's right," he said.

"By the way, how is the University of New Haven?" I asked.

"It's okay."

I didn't go into asking what his favorite subjects were. Not geography, it seemed.

When we reached my car, I said good-bye. I could have offered him a lift, but I hated the idea of even catching a fleeting glimpse of the Costanzas.

"See you tomorrow, Vincent," I said.

"Cool," he said.

When I got back into the car, I couldn't drive. I tried putting the key into the ignition, but my hand was shaking too much. I sat with the window down, a hot, smoggy breeze ruffling my hair. It seemed hard to believe that I had just been sitting across a table from my son, the product of so much love and grief and inevitably a central factor in my life. I asked myself whether I felt maternal, but I could get no answer.

Vincent and I arrived in Albuquerque on the eve of the holiday weekend and fought our way through dense airport crowds to my car, which I had left parked in the parking lot. Vincent had been craning his neck to see all he could from the plane window. The vastness of the United States seemed to take him by surprise, as did the speed of the airplane. If he had been a child, I would have taken pleasure in telling him things ("That's the Mississippi River, the longest river in America"; "Now we are over Oklahoma, the Sooner State. They called it Sooner because . . .") I like talking to children that way, but not to a tall, bumbling fellow of nineteen. I sighed when I remembered that David had been twenty-three when I first laid eyes on him, that savvy, unflappable Harvard man. And yet I couldn't say that Vincent was unintelligent. He observed, was curious, put two and two together. The concept of Environment vs. Heredity came to my mind and I promised myself to find out what the latest theories were.

The day was clear, hot, and sunny. From I-25, we could see the faraway peak of Mount Taylor. I told Vincent that it was a sacred mountain of the Navajos, and that the Americans had named it Mount Taylor after Zachary Taylor, General in the Mexican War and later President. But there were too many items in that sentence of which Vincent had obviously never heard, and I wisely let it drop. Instead, he looked around at the barren range country we were driving through, and asked, "Did you have a drought or something?"

"No, it just always looks like this. Sometimes greener, sometimes dryer, but basically this is high desert."

"Needs water."

"Some people think it's very beautiful."

"They do?" He considered this idea, then shook his head. "I like, you know, green trees, green grass."

We drove on in silence.

Presently he said, "How come you were the one that came to look for me?"

"You see, it was your grandmother's idea to send for you, and she's really too old to be running around the country by herself. She's going on eighty."

"My *nonna* from Genoa came to see us, and she's eighty-five. She helped us make like a grotto in our yard with the, you know, Virgin Mary in it. And she strung colored lights around it."

"Grandmothers differ," I said.

"But where is my—uh, father?" He could never get that word out easily, and he had not mentioned his biological mother since he'd asked me about her in New Haven.

"He's out of town. As I told you, I don't think you'll be meeting him."

"What's the matter? He doesn't like me?"

"He doesn't know you, so how could he not like you? He lives in another part of the state, and I guess maybe it's hard for him to get away. He's got a cattle ranch."

"Do you have a picture of him?"

"No." I saw that this was a blow, so I added, "I'm sure your grandparents have one."

"And one of my—uh, mother?"

"No. None of her."

He was silent a while, and then fell to reading the license plates of passing cars.

"Wow, Montana! Did you see Montana? There goes California, too." Then, tiring of that, he burst out, "I sure hope I like this grandmother. I'm kind of, you know, scared."

"Don't be, Vincent. Just mind your manners. Stand up when she comes into the room, keep your mouth closed when you chew. That kind of thing."

"You sound like my mom. What'll I talk to her about?"

"Just be natural. Talk about whatever you like to talk about."

"Ice hockey? Hunting?"

I thought, oh God, hunting. "You might talk to your Uncle Oz about hunting, but not your grandmother. She hates it."

He made a face, then scrunched down in the seat, disconsolate.

"Don't worry, Vincent. She'll do the talking, no doubt. And if you have any problems, come to me." I reached over and touched his pudgy hand, and wondered whether or not I was feeling like a mother.

159

Lydia did not permit anyone but Decatur to be present at her first interview with Vincent; I think he passed, but not with flying colors. Oz and I were invited to dinner afterward. David, it seemed, had flown to California on a voice-over assignment, and Bishy, not wanting to see David's love child until she had to, had gone somewhere to visit friends.

Lydia had made an effort to stay reasonably sober and she looked very handsome in a caftan made out of a gold-and-plum-colored sari. Vincent, in the same not-fresh Hawaiian shirt and blue jeans he had worn on the plane, had possibly washed his face. His hair was shimmery with some kind of gel he had put on it to subdue its curls. My curls. I could have told him the best way to manage them: frequent shampoos and a short haircut. I thought, if his mom were here I'm sure she would have made him take a bath. He had a sweaty smell about him. But that mother wasn't there; nor, in effect, was the other one.

"Tell us about your life, Vincent," commanded Lydia, as we began to eat one of Mrs. Martinez's especially good dinners: rib roast, Yorkshire pudding, and creamed spinach, followed by a creamy Mexican flan.

Vincent put down an overladen fork and looked wary.

"What about it?" he asked.

"Your life," repeated Lydia. "What do you do every day?"

"Get up. Eat breakfast. Jog to school. Go to classes. Come home."

"Perhaps I should have said—what do you *like* to do? What have you done lately that you enjoyed most?"

He threw me a desparate look, hesitated, then said, "Hunting. My dad took me hunting last fall. We got three deer."

"*Three* deer?" Lydia said ominously. "Three? How many do the game people allow? Surely not three?"

"Well, not exactly. It's one per license. But, well, you know."

"No, I *don't* know."

"I mean, you can go out at night and hunt with you know lights? That way, they don't catch you, if you get home before dawn."

"You flash bright lights in the animals' eyes and that blinds them, is that how it goes?"

"You got it," Vincent said.

I broke in at this point and asked him what he liked best of the subjects he was studying.

"Accounting."

I could say little about that, but Decatur suddenly stopped gazing out the window at the birds, and spoke. "Bankers in the family. Going way back. Talent for money, good thing to have."

161

"And what do you intend doing when you graduate?" Lydia pressed on.

"I've been thinking about it," Vincent said, indistinctly, because his mouth was full. "My dad does wholesale fish. I'd like helping him."

A silence pervaded the pretty dining room. A soft breeze lifted the lace curtains at the windows, which looked out toward the tallest Sangre de Cristo peaks. I wished I were up there, hiking, all by myself.

"Well, I must let you eat your dinner," Lydia said. "I'll take some more wine, Deck, if you please."

Vincent dug in. He ate rapidly and not entirely silently, while the rest of us talked about the weather forecast for the weekend, the evening news from Washington, and what to do about a new contingent of gophers in the lawn. Decatur asked where David was. Although he had been thoroughly briefed about this whole enterprise, he tended to forget parts of it.

"When's he coming home?" he persisted.

"Deck, shut up," Lydia said. "Vincent, will you have another glass of wine?"

"No thanks, ma'am," he said. "I don't like wine. I like beer."

"Oh, I see," Lydia said. She never kept beer in the house, considering it vulgar.

I began to wonder how the five of us were going

to survive the long weekend. I knew that Lydia had a schedule for Vincent—a complicated one, designed to keep him away from the general public, so that he wouldn't tell his story, but also to exhibit him to a few friends whose opinion she would later ask for. This was tricky, and in fact it proved unworkable.

Next day we took Vincent to an Indian dance, and he got talking to a girl who eventually carried him off to a barbecue party. Someone brought him home in the middle of the night, and he was discovered next morning by Filomena, asleep in the hammock, and the worse for beer. I immediately diagnosed hereditary alcholism. Lydia had better not blame this one on *me*.

But I was forgetting that in Lydia's view—and the view of her class and generation—drinking was a frivolity, a kind of joke; a failing, perhaps, but not a serious one. She was a conventional person, and she saw hard drinking as just another convention. If Vincent came home dead drunk, she did not find it blameworthy, although she would have preferred, no doubt, that he had reached that point on martinis or Scotch highballs rather than on the blue-collar drink. Stories of drunken antics had always amused her. Her code drew the line at well-bred women who lost their dignity, but nevertheless she gladly told drinking stories about women she didn't like, and even, once in a while, a story about herself when "a wee bit tiddly."

I was confident, therefore, that Vincent had not gone too far. But—who was that girl he had left the Indian dance with?

"Her name is Cherry," he told Lydia.

"*Cherry*? Good God. I don't believe I've ever heard that name before. Cherry *Who*?"

"I didn't ask her."

"Cherry. Well, Vincent, you have to watch your step a little bit here. It didn't used to be so when we first came to live in Santa Fe. Everybody knew everybody. But lately there are so many that are new."

"But so am I new. Everybody last night was real friendly. This seems like a real nice place."

Lydia decided to reminisce. "It was quite different in the Thirties. And much nicer. Your grandfather and I were the first Anglos to buy in this valley. And the Spanish people were so sweet in those days. So honest, so polite. They were all like Mrs. Martinez. But now we're seeing a flood of very peculiar newcomers—movie stars, and nouveau riche types, from places like California and Texas and God knows where. They wear two-hundred-dollar cowboy hats. And even the locals, even the Indians, have changed. That field right by our entrance used to be a beautiful chili field, but now you just see auto parts strewn all around.

Somebody's junk business. And they say the local drug dealers congregate there."

"Sounds like New Haven," Vincent said.

"But let's talk about something pleasanter," Lydia went on. "Vincent, I want you to know that I furnished this house mostly with finds from the countryside here. That chest over there was brought up from Mexico by the Gallegos family in the eighteenth century, and I bought it from their descendants. Well, of course, the ones that sold it had no idea of its value."

Vincent looked at the chest. "Real old," he pronounced, nodding wisely. He then noticed a carved madonna. "Are you guys Catholic?" he asked.

"No," Lydia replied. "We guys are not. But this old Spanish-Colonial art is absolutely charming and it's worth a lot now, too, because you can't get it anymore."

But Vincent's mind had skipped to his own interests.

"Are there any ice hockey teams here?"

Lydia did not deign to reply. She was growing weary.

"Take him to an Indian dance, Alexandra," she said. "They're dancing today at San Ildefonso. And it's time for my nap."

I thought, when will I learn to manipulate people the way she does? And why do I let her get away with it?

165

"We saw a dance yesterday," objected Vincent. "I tried to take pictures, so I could show my mom and dad, but this Indian guy wanted to charge me. Seriously, what do you see in those dances? They don't even *dance*."

"Well, Vincent, you see—" I wasn't sure how to explain this, or whether to try. "Their dancing is a very ancient form of ceremony. It's primeval. Archetypal. When we see it, we might as well be way back in Time, watching our earliest ancestors."

Vincent reflected on this and then said, "Maybe I'd like the dancing if I were in there with them. But just standing around in a crowd and, like, eyeballing it, I don't think that's so—so—"

"Primeval? You're right. The tourists and cars don't fit in."

"Can you imagine a primeval tourist?" he said, and chuckled. I was glad to see a sense of humor in him. After all, he'd been under a lot of pressure since we'd met.

Late in the day, Lydia came over to our house, leaving Vincent playing gin rummy with Deck.

"They are getting on quite well," she told us. "There seems to be a kindred spirit there."

"Don't be silly, Mother," Oz said irritably. "This kid and Pa have zilch in common. *Nada*."

"The boy has promise. Don't you agree?"

"I haven't seen a sign of it."

"What do you think, Alex?"

I wanted to stay out of it. "This is your project, Lydia," I said.

"I get very tired of always being the one to make decisions," she said, glaring at both of us. "Of course, he's frightfully common, but certain things can be changed. He's young enough to learn manners and to stop taking such enormous helpings. If we lived in Providence it would be hopeless, but here there's plenty of room for rough diamonds, don't you think? Most people here don't recognize a wrong-side-of-the-tracks New England accent. This afternoon Deck took him to the wine cellar and gave him a lesson. He'll be knowing wine in no time."

I had certainly expected that Lydia would have sent Vincent away by this time, and I found it amazing that she was sticking to her dream. Could Vincent be imagined taking over his grandfather's upper-class ways, tasting wine, wearing velvet slippers embroidered with unicorns, and speaking as if he had been to Groton and Harvard? How many years did she think it would take to turn this sow's ear into the silk purse she was looking for?

After Lydia left, I asked Oz what he thought.

"What do I think? I think this is one for David's side. Our mother is totally out to lunch. The whole idea of finding this wretched kid and dragging him out here is hare-brained."

To my surprise, I flashed back, "Wretched? I

don't think so at all. He's a nice, decent boy and I like him."

Oz looked at me with some annoyance. He got up and paced the room. "Do you really want someone like that taking over here?"

"Worse things could happen," I said. "I *like* him."

"I don't," Oz said. "You might as well go out and collar the first overweight adolescent you find on the street. Nothing special about him—just ordinary. Maybe the Glorious Light crowd are a better idea, after all."

"Oh, sure," I said, finding myself quite angry. "You'd rather have kooky strangers than David's child."

Oz threw himself down in his big chair, ignoring what I'd said, and went on, "Poor Bishy, what a rotten deal she's had. First she lost a beautiful little son, and now the only heir to carry on the Smithsons is this dumb bastard. God knows who his mother was."

"But this is all Bishy's idea," I pointed out.

"Yes, and it was a bad one, but—poor girl—she's unhappy. It's about time she left David."

"Bishy leave David? Never. It's not in her character."

"Don't be too sure. She stops in at the bank sometimes and talks to me. I can tell there's trouble going on."

I would have liked to hear more about that, but

Oz changed the subject. "By the way, David called me at the bank this morning. Wanted to know what this boy is like. I think he was relieved when I told him The Pits."

"Was he calling from California or New York?"

"Neither. That's the funny thing. He said he was in L.A., but halfway through the conversation someone came into the room where he was, to ask him something, and I heard a voice I recognized. It was Rudy—his head cowhand. Rudy's got a speech defect, a sort of lisp. You can't miss it. I know, because I've talked to him on the phone several times. It was Rudy, all right, so David must have been home at the ranch."

So, I thought. David is hiding. And some part of him really cares about his son, or he wouldn't have telephoned.

+ VII +

On the Tuesday after Memorial Day weekend, I was the one to take Vincent to the airport. I could tell that things had not gone well with Lydia, because she did not come out of the house to see him off. Decatur came shambling along, offered his hand, grinned, clapped Vincent on the back. But I'm not sure that he knew to whom he was saying good-bye. In a stylish old man like Decatur, manners are the last component to disintegrate. On the last day of his life he will stand up if a lady enters the room.

"Good-bye, my boy. It's been a great pleasure to have you with us."

"Bye," said Vincent, and hopped into the car. Manners were as easy for him as for Decatur, though in an opposite way: he simply omitted them entirely.

For about twenty miles on I-25, Vincent had

nothing to say at all. He sat beside me like a large stuffed animal.

Finally he said, "I need your advice."

"I'll do my best."

He peered around at me with his wide, earnest eyes. "How can I get out of this?"

I felt like laughing, but of course nothing was funny. "Do you mean, out of inheriting a million-dollar property?"

"Yeah."

"You can just say you don't want it."

"I did. I told the old lady that. But she got sort of, like, mad."

"Never mind if she got mad. It's your right to decide your own life. But are you sure?"

"Sure I'm sure. I don't like it here. I asked if my mom and dad could move out here with me if I accepted and she said no."

"Hmm."

Vincent sighed. Then he looked at me imploringly and said, "Alex, I was hoping I'd at least *see* my father."

"Well, you know, Vincent, I told you—"

"But *why* doesn't he want to see me?"

"I don't know. Maybe he would find it too painful. I doubt that he just doesn't give a damn."

"Where is he?"

"At his ranch, I guess."

"Do you like him?"

"Yes," I said, and felt rather surprised to hear that.

We continued to drive toward Albuquerque in silence. I noticed that Vincent was sweating, and I said, "It's getting hotter. When we leave Santa Fe and start going downhill the temperature rises. Albuquerque is two thousand feet lower."

But he didn't seem to have been listening to me. He was looking miserable.

"Listen, Alex," he said. "Are you my friend? Then take me to see my father."

"Oh, Vincent—"

"No, look, I mean it. I'll never be back here again, and I just want to have seen him. I mean, don't you think he owes me something? After all, he HAD me."

"It was your mother who had you, Vincent," I pointed out gently.

"But he sure had a lot to do with it. Alex, I'm asking you. I think I'll hate him, but I just want to meet him."

"It's about a two-hour drive. You'll miss your plane."

"We'll call up and cancel."

"It won't be easy to get another seat today— right after the long weekend."

"I don't care how long it takes." He looked at me beseechingly. "Don't say no," he said.

So that was how it happened. When we reached

the intersection of Route I-40, I turned east. Common sense suggested to me that David might not be there; that instead I'd find Bishy; or both of them. But now I knew I had to do this and that it would be a mistake to phone and say we were coming because then David would surely disappear. And suddenly, I also knew something else: I, too, wanted to see David.

When we reached the first small town, Vincent asked me to turn off the highway. He wanted, he said, to buy something: a souvenir. At his request, we found a hardware store, and Vincent went in alone, returning with a large paper bag. He did not volunteer any comments, nor did I make any. About an hour later, we stopped for gas, and Vincent treated me to a Coke. I told him that was kind of him and he smiled for the first time on this journey.

"I'm real nervous," he said.

"Of course you are. So am I."

"You? Why should *you* be nervous?"

Although I couldn't explain, I told him what was certainly true: "Because I don't know what's ahead of us here and I want the best for you."

To my surprise, he leaned over and gave me a kiss on the cheek. "You're nice," he said.

After that we talked but little. We were now on a two-lane road that ran straight across grazing country. On either side of the road we passed herds of cattle, always congregated around one of the scarce shade trees. Typical New Mexico clouds, like small, uniform puffs of very white smoke, gave some definition to the otherwise limitless blue sky. In the rear-view mirror I could see the eastern slopes of the Sangre de Cristo Mountains near Santa Fe, colored green, gray, and misty blue.

"Look behind you, Vincent," I said. "Beautiful New Mexico."

"Yeah," he said. "But, like, empty. I never saw anything so empty. I could never live here."

"Lucky for you, you don't have to," I said.

I had never been to David's ranch, but, more than once over the years, I had studied the road map to find the little town it was near. When we reached that town, I inquired at a gas station if anyone knew where the Smithson Ranch was, and someone did: five miles farther, on the right. "Look for the blue gate."

Here on the high plains, the wind was much rowdier than in Santa Fe. During the twenty minutes it took to reach the blue gate, gusts began to sweep across the range, so that tiny volleys of dust struck the windshield and our faces. I thought, Bishy would have to love either ranching or David very much to put up with this. Does she? And which one?

The blue gate, which Vincent got out of the car

to open and close, led onto a dirt road that continued for several miles. Finally we saw the ranch
house in the distance, set among cottonwoods.
Not far from it we passed a corral where cowhands
were breaking a young horse.

"It's a cattle ranch, Vincent," I said. "Not like
Gallegos Ranch."

"Why don't the Smithsons have animals?"

"Too much trouble. They lease some acreage to
farmers, but that's about it."

"Then why have all that land?"

I thought for a minute. "Prestige, maybe."

"Why do they need prestige?"

"You ask good questions, Vincent. I hope you'll
take a course in sociology."

We passed an old, windowless adobe barn with
doors that were closed and barred.

"What's that for?"

"I don't know. Storage, maybe."

"That big old blank wall makes me think of a
clean blackboard. All ready to write on."

Later, I was to remember that rather curious
remark. Now, we were close to the ranch house,
and a pickup truck outside suggested that someone
was at home. I glanced at Vincent's face and found
that it looked more adult than at any time since we
had met. Adult and determined.

"Here we are," I said. "How do you want to do
this?"

He said firmly, "I've got a plan. You go in and see if he's there and if he'll see me. If he won't, I'll just go on in anyway."

"Okay," I said. "But give me some time."

"Ten minutes. Then I'm coming in."

I opened the unlocked screen door and let myself into a cluttered entryway, full of coats and boots. It led directly into a big living room, and there I saw David, his back to me, sitting at a rolltop desk. I knocked and he looked around and saw me and jumped to his feet, obviously shocked.

"Sorry if I startled you," I said.

"My God, Alex, I don't believe it. What in the world—?"

"I have to talk to you."

"Come on in." He walked toward me slowly. Then he held out his hands and I took them. Then he kissed me on each cheek.

"I don't believe it," he said again. He led me toward chairs and a sofa in front of a big stone fireplace. "Would you like a drink?"

"Thanks, but I have to drive back to Santa Fe. This is a short visit."

"I guess you're here to lecture me about my custody suit, but whatever mean things you are about to say, I'm glad you came. I want you to know that right now."

One part of my mind was telling me that there was a lot of gray in his dark hair and that he looked tired and his eyes were sad, but that he was still a man whom I found remarkably attractive. Another part was urging me to get on at once with my mission.

"David," I said, "someone is with me, waiting in the car. He wants very very much to see you. Vincent Costanza."

Right away he backed off from me, shaking his head. "You know I don't want to see him, Alex."

"But he wants to see you so badly. Just this once, just for a couple of minutes, David. Suppose you had never met *your* father! Come on, try to put yourself in the boy's place."

"He should put himself in *my* place."

"Why should he? Did *he* start this?"

For the first time, David smiled slightly. "No, he didn't," he said. "I'm the one. I fell in love with you."

I must have looked shaken, because I had not expected that, or anything else about the two of us. Or had I? Had I even been hoping for it?

"We have so many things to say to each other," he said. "Sit down and let's talk."

"It wouldn't be a good idea. It's Vincent I want you to talk to."

"Suppose I go outside and just say hello to him. *Then* can we talk?"

"For a couple of minutes."

"For an hour. I'll send him down to the corral to see the horses."

"*Half* an hour," I said, with misgivings. "But go and see Vincent right now."

I waited, sitting on Bishy's Bostonian-looking slipcovered sofa and holding a cat that jumped up in my lap. I felt like an intruder in Bishy's house, but at the same time I noticed, and took pleasure in disliking, the pattern she had chosen for her slipcovers. It was a print showing women in hoop-skirts and bonnets, chatting with gentlemen in high collars. The people appeared every eight inches or so and between them were trails of ribbons and bowknots. Sentimental. Affected. Just like Bishy, I thought.

After less than ten minutes, I saw Vincent drive past the window in my car, and David returned to the house. He looked grim.

I said, "What happened?"

David said, "If you'd known what he really wanted to do, I don't think you would have brought him here. He just wanted to tell me what a son-of-a-bitch I am."

"That's all? I'm sorry."

"Mostly he just stared at me. I said I hoped he understood why I didn't want to meet him—that it was of course nothing I have against him, just that both our lives will work better without the other one. Then I told him I needed to talk family busi-

181

ness with you and why didn't he go down to the corral and watch the guys break in the colt. And then he called me a son of a bitch and a cop-out." David went over to the bar and poured himself a tot of whiskey, which he tossed off neat. "Don't worry, I'm not a drunk—not yet—but I wouldn't mind about six more of those. And do you know why? Because Vincent is right."

I said, "Vincent thinks you didn't want him, but he doesn't know you never had a chance to want him. Or *not* want him."

David, who was standing near me, in front of the fireplace, abruptly turned his head away. "Guilt," he said, after a pause. "I've had two sons and I'm drowned in guilt about both of them."

I could think of nothing to say, no way to help him, until he added, "And guilt about you. All that happened to you."

Quickly, I said, "I'm fine now. And Vincent will be fine. I understand about the guilt. I'm not telling you never to feel any, but give yourself a rest."

He came over to sit beside me on the sofa. "That's hard," he said.

"I know."

"Back then, a million bucks went down the drain and it was my own crazy fault. And then Mother and Dad were leaning on me to marry

Bishy. But I can't say they forced me. I was the one at the altar."

"David," I said. "There's no point in going back over all that."

"Yes, there is, because, Alex, I loved you. I truly loved you. I guess I like to think that if I'd known you were pregnant I'd have asked Bishy for a divorce and you and I would have been married. But I can't honestly be sure."

"It wouldn't have happened." I remembered what Bishy had said to me that New Year's morning in the kitchen, and I added, "She'd have told you it wouldn't be good for you."

"Anyway," David went on, "I was what Dad calls a whippersnapper. Too full of myself. Too young, too dumb. I failed you."

"No," I said, laying my hand gently, for an instant, on his shirtsleeve. "David, we were *two* young, dumb whippersnappers."

This conversation, I thought, should be kept as light as possible, but the mood of it had changed since love had been mentioned. I wanted to say how glad I was to hear that he had truly loved me, and to tell him how overwhelmingly I had loved him, and perhaps still did. But, as usual, I was cautious and held back. After a minute, I said in a cheery tone, "But, come on, let's not put ourselves down too much. It was a fine time, back then. We made it that way. It's a good memory."

"Is that all it is?"

I folded my arms, to keep from touching him again. "Tell me about your life here, David. What interests you?"

He made an effort and said, "I try to keep this ranch going, but I'm not a very good cattleman. I do some voice-overs still, but the truth is, if you don't live in New York or L.A., they forget about you. I hate it, anyway. It makes me feel like a nonperson. I've been drawing lately. You remember, in college I used to draw a lot. I don't feel like cartoons, though. Maybe things don't strike me as very funny anymore."

"Draw what comes."

"Alex, I wish I could do what you want me to do about Vincent. To make you happy, if nothing else."

"Maybe you'll feel like it someday," I said. "It's not as if he were alone in the world, you know. I'd feel very sad about him, but he has loving parents and he enjoys life."

"Does he know exactly *who* you are?"

"No, only you and I know that. But I'm beginning to think I'll tell him someday."

"Maternal instinct?"

"Maybe so. Oz thinks he's hopeless and Lydia thinks he needs a lot of work, but I like him. He's perceptive, too. He knows better than to be impressed with people like Lydia and Deck."

"Good. Very promising," David said. "Tell him I very much hope we'll eventually get to be friends. Alex, I would like to kiss you."

I moved away from him. "Let's be smart," I said. "Let's leave things alone."

"Why? Things are bad," he said. "Things need changing. Why do you think I went to court over the Gallegos Ranch? Because I can't stand my life. Neither can Bishy stand hers. I wanted to get my half of the inheritance and sell it. So that Bishy and I could be divorced and get out of here."

I was silent, nonplussed by this news.

He said, "How do you and Oz get along?"

"Okay," I said faintly.

"When I heard, back then, that you two were together again and getting married, I felt desperate. I hoped you'd call me and tell me yourself. Didn't you even think of calling me?"

I hesitated and then I said, "Yes, I certainly did think of it, but I wouldn't let myself do it. Bishy was pregnant. You and I had nothing to say to each other."

"We had everything to say to each other, but— you're right—we probably wouldn't have said it." Then he went on in a toneless voice, "You can't imagine how awful I felt that summer before, when you disappeared out of New York. I asked the superintendent of that building you lived in—and the postman—and the neighbors. None of them

185

knew where you'd gone. Then Mother told me that you'd broken the engagement and Oz didn't know how to reach you. Alex, I never even imagined a baby."

"Oz knew I'd gone abroad. He didn't tell you that?"

"No. We don't talk much, you know. Never did. There's not a lot of brotherly love flowing between us."

"Well, I guess that's pretty clear."

"Once, when we were teenagers, we were hunting together up around Chama. We'd been quarreling —we often quarreled—and he got furious. I walked on ahead. We hadn't seen any deer yet, and I had just caught sight of a white tail. I wasn't thinking about anything except how to get closer to it. And all of a sudden, Oz's rifle went off and a bullet went by my head and hit a tree about eight inches away. I looked around and saw Oz standing there staring at me. He said, 'Jesus, David, it just went off.' And he kept saying, 'It just went of by *itself*.' And then he unloaded the rifle, and dropped all the bullets on the ground, and then he turned around and headed for where we'd left our car. I didn't even try to follow him. I waited a while and then I walked back to Chama another way and hitched a ride to Santa Fe."

"My God, David."

"Now, I'm not saying he did it on purpose. I'll

never know. Maybe *he* doesn't know. But after that, we stopped the stupid quarrels. We stopped being kids, and we had as little to do with each other as possible."

"And you two never talked about it?"

"Never."

"Poor Oz," I said. "Before we were married, I tried to tell him about the baby—leaving you out—but he said he didn't want to hear my secrets and he didn't want to tell me his."

"He doesn't know why you went to Europe?"

"No, and let's keep it that way."

"Do you love him, Alex?"

I said, "I don't think that's your business."

He gave me a searching look. "You're not going to tell me how you feel about him?"

"No," I told him, although I realized that I wanted to say volumes more. "I have to be going. Vincent just drove in, I think."

"Don't go. I need to tell you about the custody suit."

I said, "That's hardly in the forefront of my mind just now."

"Or of mine, either. But—just to let you know—I've withdrawn it."

I was surprised to note how little I cared. "How come?"

"Because it seems that Dad doesn't have a clear title to the Gallegos Ranch, and never did. Whether he tries to give it to the Glorious Lighters or leaves it in the family, the title is so messed up that the Gallegos family may be real heirs, but I doubt they'll take us to court. We'd all be there for the next twenty years. There are something like ninety-five Gallegos heirs."

"So we might have been spared all this."

"Yep. But no one knew that. I only found it out when I had the title searched."

"I'm glad it turned out this way," I said. "Now maybe everything can get back to normal."

"Normal? What's that? You mean, Ma and Pa drinking themselves into zombies? And Bishy and I looking for a way to never see each other again? Of course, I don't know about you and Oz, but it's possible he's boring you to death."

"Maybe *I* bore *him*," I said. "I wish I could talk to Oz better. Find out what he's feeling—what he wants—"

David looked surprised. "What *he* wants? What about you? What do *you* want?"

I stared at him, feeling very much as I had felt when Dr. Fischer asked about my epitaph: would it simply record that I had been polite and eager to please? It occurred to me that the recent extraordinary events had changed me. I rejected the epitaph. David's question, "What do *you* want?" seemed exceedingly pertinent.

"You're right," I said. "Oz has his rights, but so do I. I need to make some decisions."

"I hope I'll be the first to know," David said.

"But all I'm sure of right now is that I have to get Vincent to the airport." And I stood up to leave.

David stood up, too, and put his arms around me. He kissed me, and we kissed each other, and I think several minutes went by.

"God," David said softly. "I remember so much about you."

"David, I really *must* go. I promise, I'll be in touch."

"Be in touch? That sounds pretty offhand. When? In another twenty years?"

"No. Sooner than that. How about next week?"

"How about tomorrow?"

"No," I said. "We need thinking time. We're not the same people we were twenty years ago."

"We're nicer," he said.

"Promise to *think*," I said, and left him.

Outside, I got into the driver's seat of my car, beside Vincent, and we drove off. I found Vincent taciturn, and it seemed to me that he might have been crying. Not wanting to invade his privacy, I, too, was quiet. That is, until we passed the storage barn. There I nearly sent the car into the ditch as I slammed on the brakes. Written in enormous, spray-painted letters, all over the side of the barn, was this sentence: DAVID SMITHSON WHERE IS YOUR WANDERING SPERM TONIGHT?

My feelings were so seriously confused that I could think of nothing to say. I was angry, sad, outraged, sympathetic, and even, perhaps, a bit amused. But, above all, I had had enough shocks for one day.

"Well?" Vincent finally said.

"Well?" I said.

"I hate him. That's why I bought the spray paint. I knew I would hate him. I'm sorry if you're mad at me."

I said, "Does this make you feel better?"

"I think so."

"Well, I hope so. I'd hate to think we came all this way and that you went to all that work with the spray paint, just so you would feel worse. But Vincent! I know you think now that you hate him, but that could change. Believe me!"

He gave me a wavering smile. "If you say so," he said. "You're my friend."

"Of course I am, and don't forget it. You're a good guy."

"If it hadn't been for you, Alex," he said, "I couldn't have stood it here."

Tears came to my eyes, and I thought, I'll surely tell him someday, but this isn't the time.

I called Oz from the little town near David's ranch, so that he wouldn't worry about my coming home late.

He sounded annoyed. "Where the hell are you?"

I thought of lying—of pretending that Vincent's plane was hours late and that I was still at the airport—but it seemed to me that, at this point, the more truth the better.

"Vincent wanted to see David," I said. "So I drove him there. Now I'm taking him to Albuquerque."

Oz said, "Well, that was a dumb thing to do. I told you David didn't want to see him."

"But Vincent wanted to see *him*."

"Alex, you're always letting yourself be pushed around by bossy people. When are you going to learn?"

"Maybe right away," I said.

"I certainly hope so."

"You may not like it."

"I'll love it. Alex, I've had a hard day. If I'm asleep when you get home, don't wake me."

"I will if I must," I said. It seemed an odd thing to say, but I said it.

"What?"

"Didn't you hear me?"

"No. It sounded like 'I will if I must.' "

"That's right," I said. "Bye, Oz."

I got home before nine and Oz was still up. I had had plenty of time to think, while driving from the airport, and I now knew what I must do, although I wasn't sure how to do it, and I feared it might take months. Or years.

I had worked out several opening gambits, but Oz forestalled them by saying, "Good news. Mother had a call from her lawyer to say that David has withdrawn his suit. So now she's decided to change the will back so that the ranch comes to her sons. End of nightmare."

"I'm very glad," I said.

"Now we need to get back to normal," he said, looking at me critically. "You've been behaving in a strange way, Alex. What did you mean when you said you'd wake me if you *must*?"

"I meant that I'd wake you if I needed to talk to you."

"That doesn't sound very considerate. One thing I always liked about you, you were considerate, but now you seem to be getting selfish. And, Alex, I have to say, it was very wrong of you to take that boy to see David."

"I'm glad I did," I said.

"He could cause a lot of trouble for David. Not to mention Bishy. He could keep bobbing up—wanting money, no doubt."

"He won't. I *know* he won't. Give me some credit for knowing something once in a while."

"Not when you're wrong," he said firmly. "But it's done, so I'll say no more. Now, then: what was it you wanted to talk to me about that's so important?"

I took a deep breath. "Marriage. *This* marriage. Things we've never talked about in eighteen years."

I thought this might bring on the wary captain look, but instead he seemed somewhat relieved. "Oh," he said. "I thought it might be about a particular thing."

"What particular thing were you thinking of?"

"Nothing at all important," he said. "It's just that two of your friends saw me having lunch with Bishy the other day, and they kept looking at us. So I thought maybe they'd told you."

"Why should they?" I asked.

"Only because one of them happened to see me lunching with her before. You know Santa Fe. People love to gossip, particularly when a woman is as good-looking as Bishy. I wouldn't want you to feel hurt."

"I thought Bishy went to visit friends—to avoid Vincent."

"The friends she's visiting live here."

I said I wasn't hurt, and perhaps I said it so convincingly that I hurt *him*.

"As I've told you before," he said huffily, "she's a wonderful woman and she's had a wretched time. You can't imagine—"

"She seems to have made you her confidant."

"She asks for my advice." And after a pause, he added, "Which is more than you've ever done."

Then, quite suddenly, he went off into tirades

about how detached I always was and how uninterested in him, and how I was never home because I was taking useless courses, and how tired he was of being thrown hand-knit sweaters as if they could make up for all that was missing.

Now I did begin to feel hurt, because I hadn't thought our marriage was that bad. But he was right about the sweaters. No matter how intricate the pattern or how long it took me to knit them, he needed love instead.

What he was saying caught me completely off guard. I had anticipated a painful dialogue, initiated by me. And that after many hours and thousands of unhappy words, we would agree to give our marriage another try—say, for a year or more. Instead, I now felt as if I had mounted a horse known for its plodding gait and suddenly found myself racing off across rough prairie, heading for the horizon.

I don't know, and don't wish to know, the full story about those lunches with Bishy, although helpful friends let me know that there had been dinners, too, and that someone had once seen them in a parked car near Nambe Falls. For me, these occasions had served an important purpose: they had brought Oz to look at our relationship and find it wanting. I respected him for doing so. And it was clear to both of us that we had come to the end of our marriage.

*   *   *

A week later, I was packing. Oz would continue to live in the house, so I packed everything that belonged to me and left no trace of myself—exactly as my mother used to do. For sentiment, I kept two of the Thai lacquer finger bowls, but I sent the other twenty-two to my sister, whose husband had recently been named Ambassador to Bolivia. One of the many decisions I had reached was that I did not need finger bowls.

I called David and told him what had happened, and that I felt I ought to go away by myself for a while and think things through; also, that I had bought a ticket to Rome.

"I'm coming with you," he said.

"Not now."

"When?"

"When each of us has sorted everything out."

"I am completely sorted out."

"But I'm changing, David. When you knew me, I used to do everything your way. I doubt if I will anymore, and you may not like it."

"Try me," he said. "Alex! For God's sake, don't disappear on me."

"I won't."

"I'm coming to Rome."

"Oh, no!" I said in alarm. "I'll write and I'll telephone. It's just that I ought to think things over. Don't you believe in caution?"

"At a time like this? What we need now is no caution whatsoever. Total recklessness."

I thought of my cautious father and my anxious mother, and Ginevra feeding her automatic baby. I decided to say no more about caution.

"It's just that I've been facing in one direction for so many years and now everything has whirled around. Including me." I paused, trying to think how to explain this better. "I feel as if I must put a puzzle together. A complicated jigsaw puzzle that I've never done before."

"I can help you," he said. "I like puzzles."

"But you can't do this one. It's mine."

After that, he was silent. Finally he said, "Well, darling Alex, whatever you want."

"It won't take long," I said, beginning to waver. "Not long at all, probably. We'll have to see."

Flying across the Atlantic, I felt the way I had felt as a child: wondering why I was traveling, but aware that the home I was leaving had vanished, and there could be no going back. Then, at least, I had my parents with me, but now, no one. I had called David just before it was time to board the plane, to say another good-bye and promise to write, but he wasn't at the ranch. I thought about calling him now, from the plane, but I said to myself, if you're flying off by yourself to demonstrate that you are brave and independent and

196

don't just do things to please people, then stick to it.

I dozed for a while and then woke up with an absolute conviction: I was doing this not to be brave and self-directing, but because I was a cautious mouse. To go back to David might be inadvisable (or not), but it was what I wanted. I couldn't spend my life holding back and running away, especially not from love. This, I told myself, is going to be the shortest visit to Rome anyone ever made.

When the plane landed and I had been through the passport check and customs, I asked the porter to take me to the ticket counter, where I planned to change my return flight to an earlier one. But at the place where the passengers' friends and relatives were waiting for them, all my loneliness and every vestige of indecision went away for good. I knew I was home at last. David had met the plane.

MARY CABLE was born in Cleveland, Ohio, and brought up in Providence, Rhode Island. After a number of years in New York and in various foreign countries, she now lives in Santa Fe, New Mexico.

A recipient of grants from both the National Endowment for the Arts and the National Endowment for the Humanities, she has written several books on aspects of American social history, including *Top Drawer*, and *The Blizzard of '88*. She has also served as an editor/writer for *The New Yorker*, *Harper's Bazaar*, *American Heritage*, and *Horizon*.

Tell Me the Truth About Love is her second novel.